The Slave,
the Hunter,
the Missionary
and
the Smous

First publication 2018 by Footprints Press, South Africa

Website: www.hiltonbarber.co.za

Copyright © David Hilton-Barber 2018

Cover design and page layout by Anthony Cuerden
Email: ant@flyingant.co.za

Illustrations by Lidia Milne
Email: lidia.milne99@gmail.com

Printed by Pinetown Printers (Pty) Ltd

ISBN: 978-0-6399326-7-5

The Slave,
the Hunter,
the Missionary
and
the Smous

By David Hilton-Barber

Introduction

The short story has taken its place in literature as a distinct genre and can encompass parable, myth, folktale and anecdote. It often speaks simply of important things or, conversely, reveals importance in trivia. Frank O'Connor, an Irish writer of over 150 works, best known for his short stories and memoirs, and whose name is commemorate in the O'Connor International Short Story Award, observed that the short story has never had a hero.

This has particular relevance to the short story in South Africa, according to Jean Marquard[1], where many of these describe the 'unremarkable struggles of people in a harsh and bureaucratic society.'

She goes on to write: 'The reasons for this are historical just as much as they are artistic, since English-speaking South Africa is quintessentially a society without heroes.'

The short story writer may not consciously choose his audience – he may be writing for himself or, like Horace, for posterity. His attitude to his reader may be one of condescension or even hostility. He may assume his reader has a liberal education, a sense of humour or, in general terms, someone who is merely seeking entertainment and possibly enlightenment.

As a writer of mainly South African non-fiction historical works, my intention with this volume of short stories is to portray something of the life and times of ordinary people in the Cape and beyond; how they coped with the often harsh conditions of their day, and how the events of that time have with some relevance to present-day challenges.

David Hilton-Barber

---

1 Editor of *A Century of South African Short Stories*, AD Donker, 1978

Contents

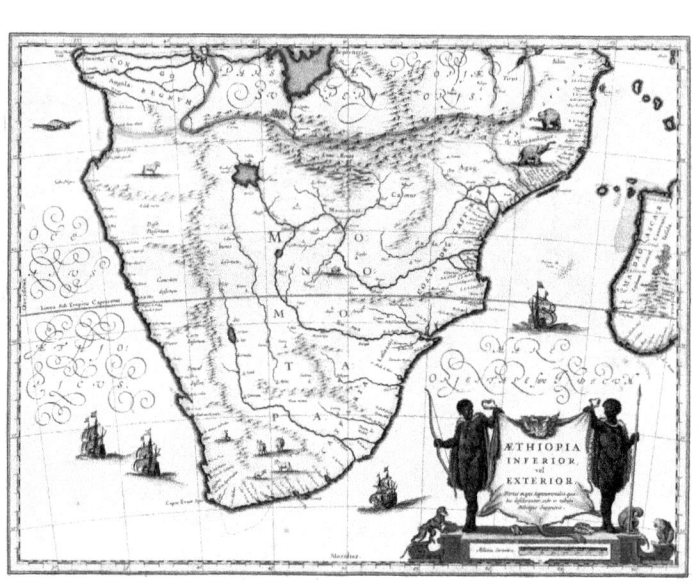

Gerrit and Helena Bas

Gerrit de Goede was born in the Dutch village of Bergen-op-Zoom in the middle years of the 18th Century. His father considered him sufficiently well-educated at the age of 16 to offer him to the East India Company's service. How else could a youth from a common but honest family achieve advancement in what was in many respects an arm of government engaged in colonising and ruling immense territories overseas? The Company, which already had more men of ability than the civil service of the mother country, engaged Gerrit under a five year contract to act in whatever capacity he should be found most competent. Several of his friends from school were also taken into the Company's service. Gerrit was posted to the Cape and sailed out of Rotterdam on the vessel Terhorst. His first position, he was told, was as junior clerk in the office of the secretary of the Council of Policy.

He was not to know it but he had arrived at the Cape at a crucial time. On the very vessel that brought him was a memorandum from the Directors of the Company. This reflected the worries of the Chambers of Amsterdam, Zeeland and the other business communities in Holland. They were concerned as to the future course of development that should be followed. In this memorandum, the Directors asked each member of the Council, which included the Governor, the Secunde, the fiscal independent, the commander of the garrison and a number of junior members, to give serious consideration to a number of questions. The matters to be discussed were to affect the entire future development of South Africa, and to sow the seeds for the strife and conflict of the next two and a half centuries.

Gerrit's superior, whom he was yet to meet, Mynheer van Hoorn, personally delivered the sealed package to the Governor that same afternoon. Within a few days, the contents were widely known to the officials of the Company. At a Council meeting to be called six months hence, every member was required to give a comprehensive report on each of the questions raised. The principal queries were whether the country could maintain a large number of colonists, whether it would not be more advantageous to employ European labourers than slaves and what articles which were in demand in the mother country could be produced. These included coffee, sugar, cotton, indigo, olive oil, tobacco, flax, silk and hops. But the real nub of the problem, as everyone knew, centred on the moral issue of slaves. The council members were believed to have sufficient wisdom and foresight to give proper consideration to this matter.

"Do you have an opinion on slavery?" Mynheer van Hoorn asked Gerrit. They were waiting on the dockside to board the *Postlooper* which had arrived that morning from Holland en route to Mauritius and thence the Far East.

"Sir, I knew little of the matter." Gerrit hesitated. "We were always told that slavery was a malignant sore in the human frame."

"Strong words," van Hoorn answered. "I agree that slavery was a serious moral issue. Nevertheless, a lot of people, both in Holland and in the Cape, feel that black people were destined to be slaves."

"The emancipation of slaves could surely be justified in the civilised norms of Europe," Gerrit said.

The gangplank was finally secured and they went on board. Gerrit remained on deck while his master entered the captain's cabin. He was shocked to see a young black maiden crying pathetically on deck. Being a compassionate youth and sensing an opportunity to exercise gallantry, he attempted to speak to her in comforting terms, and asked if there was perhaps something he could do to stem the flow of tears. But the girl covered her face with her hands and wailed even more sorrowfully. He took out his handkerchief and offered it to her. Finally, she brought her crying to a halt and dabbed her eyes with the fine linen cloth.

Mynheer van Hoorn emerged from the cabin with a handful of documents. He noticed Gerrit's concern for the young woman. "Let me tell you the background to this particular little human drama." Gerrit listened while he related the sad story. "Her previous owner, a wealthy Maria Bas, brought her back from India where she had been taken on as a slave girl and worked for five years as her waiting maid. But on their return to the Netherlands, it soon became clear that Madame Bas could no longer make use of her services and she is being returned to Mauritius, an island which has recently been abandoned by the East India Company as a station of .refreshment. She was the daughter of a slave woman employed by the Company in India. Her mother had originally come from Mauritius but had since died. Helena knows no one in Mauritius and was desperately miserable at the prospect of leaving her erstwhile employer who had shown her nothing but kindness since she had been taken in by the Bas family. Now, what awaits her in Mauritius?"

He showed Gerrit a document signed by the directors to the effect that the holder, one Helena Bas, was to be treated as a free person with all the rights pertaining to that station. This was the standard letter of emancipation.

"She speaks Dutch fluently, according to the captain," van Hoorn stated. The two men observed her as she stared across the railing towards the shore. "Ask her," said Gerrit, whether she wants to stay here in the Cape."

Van Hoorn posed the question but the girl remained silent. Finally she gained confidence and after further coaxing, she confirmed that she would like to remain there but was told it was not permitted.

Gerrit went back to the ship in the afternoon to speak to Helena. The captain told him she had been confined to one of the cabins for the period the ship was in harbour. "I need to speak to her about her papers," Gerrit said. The captain laughed out loud. "Speak to her? I know what she's good for. She'll know the size of my speaker before very long." He pronounced the word "spyker" which is the common word for a nail. "Carry on, my lad. Tell her to prepare herself for the on-voyage to Mauritius."

Gerrit blushed and turned away. He followed the rating down to the lower deck and took the key from him. "I will return this shortly," he said. Helena Bas was sitting on the small bunk. She leaped up when he entered. Gerrit put his hands on her shoulders. He was trembling. "Listen, Helena. Do you want to go back to Mauritius?"

"You know I do not. I know no one there. There is nowhere for me to stay. There is no work. What will I do?"

"I will try to help you."

Gerrit confronted van Hoorn the next morning. "Mynheer, I must speak to you about Helena Bas. Surely with your influence you could take up the matter with the Company? There should be no reason, as a freed person, why

Helena could not seek a position with the Company in the Cape and I myself could see to her well-being. The *Postlooper* is due to remain at Table Bay for another week before proceeding around the point and up the Indian Ocean to Mauritius and thence on to Java. Have we not time to get an alternative dispensation for her?"

Until then, Gerrit's experience with people of colour had been confined to the handful of Indonesian and Indian school friends. He held the conventional view that blacks were first enslaved on the plea that they were heathens. Just as soon as they were converted to Christianity, and had acquired a working knowledge of the Dutch language, then they could expect freedom and be placed on a level with their former masters in terms of civil rights.

"My dear fellow," Mynheer van Hoorn said. "We in the Cape are very reluctant to allow emancipation to any but a special few. And even then, security must be given by the owner that the freed person should not become a charge upon the poor funds within ten years. More and more of our people are of the view that slavery is the proper condition of the black race. Habits of industry, which in Europeans are the result of pressure of circumstances operating upon the race through hundreds of generations, are found to be opposed to the disposition of Africans. In most instances, emancipation means the conversion of a useful individual into an indolent pauper and a pest to society."

Gerrit was profoundly taken aback. "But this maiden is surely not in that category. You yourself stated that she has worked in a European household for more than five years. She appears to be diligent and has undoubtedly picked up the proper habits of industry, as you term it."

"No, my lad. Experience has shown that a freed slave usually chooses to live in a filthy hovel upon coarse and scanty food rather than toil for something better. Decent clothing is not a necessity of life and no furniture is needed in the hovel other than a few cooking utensils."

What an indictment on the civilising influence that the Company purported to wield, Gerrit thought. The discussion with his superior continued most of that day. Mynheer van Hoorn was a moral and educated person, Gerrit knew. How could he hold these prejudiced views? Gerrit persisted. "The Directors ask whether this country should be occupied solely by Europeans or whether there should be a mixture of races in it. Is it not that they favour the former view? After all, apart from the few hundred Hottentots living nearby, whom the Company seeks to protect by banning any contact between them and the burghers, there are only a small number of slaves here, nearly five-sixths of whom are adult males. Slavery has not taken deep root and we could easily do away with it. Without any further importations, the system will rapidly perish."

"This is not the view of the Council" Van Hoorn laughed. "No, indeed it is not. The majority of the members, I vouch, are incapable of looking beyond the gains of the present hour. Their view is that a slave costs less than three pounds a year for maintenance, whereas a white labourer would cost at least as much as a soldier, whose pay and rations amount to more than twelve pounds a year. These people aver that the slave is tractable whereas the European is prone to be rebellious. White men often become addicted to drunkenness, especially that sort who would be prepared to perform the severest form of manual labour in this climate."

"And will the view of these Council members prevail?"

"Unfortunately, yes. And unfortunately a lot of what they say is true. But there is also a strong minority view that holds that the condition of slavery distorts the whole life of the colony. Their view is that the burghers are kept in a state of unrest through slavery. The slaves themselves, notwithstanding the terrible punishments inflicted upon them, are not deterred from running away and committing atrocious crimes. To those that hold this point of view, even the economic argument does not make sense. A slave costs three or four pounds, and even if the maintenance costs are low, one has to add the cost of bringing him to the country and guarding him. They require close supervision too, at the work place. Taking all this into consideration, they are not all that much cheaper than Europeans."

Gerrit shook his head sadly. "Mark my words, sir. The introduction of negro slaves to the Cape will produce many evils the consequences of which will be felt long after the present council members have themselves left this mortal state."

The young de Goede hated this aspect of his job with the Company. He felt brutalised by the conditions which prevailed. He thought that the punishments meted out were barbarous in the extreme. "Why does a civilised country like Holland allow its citizens to behave in such an uncivilized manner?" he asked van Hoorn. "Some of the death sentences transcend all human decency. I cannot stand it."

"The law must be enforced, even if the methods appear to you to be harsh. The constituted authority of the country cannot be defied. Otherwise the people would refuse to pay taxes and generally evade the laws."

"But to get back to the circumstance of Helena Bas. What can we do?"

"Nothing, my lad. Nothing."

Late in the afternoon Gerrit went back to the *Postlooper* with great despondency. He told Helena that he had been unsuccessful. She burst into tears. "Then I will run away. I cannot stay here on this ship. That captain...." She did not finish. Gerrit took her in his arms. He realized for the first time that she was comely. Her eyes were beautifully black and as clear and pure as those of a wild bird. No matter that her noses were flattened. Her teeth were clean and white, her hands well-shaped, her fingers long, her legs shapely, her feet small and pretty. Helena was nervous and she pushed him gently away. Gerrit was unsure of himself. He needed time to think. "I will come back in the morning," he said. But he never did. Whether consciously or not, he left the cabin door unlocked when he departed.

"Look at this," van Hoorn said. It was several months later. He was paging through some official papers on his desk. "Your friend Helena Bas has been apprehended. She appears in court this morning on a charge of assault."

"Assault?" de Goede asked. "I can hardly believe that." He tried to remain calm but his mind was racing. Helena, Helena. He had done nothing to alleviate her plight and was racked with guilt. But what could he have done?

"It states here that she has been working for a burgher family and raised her hand in defence against her employer, one Frans van Nierop, when he attempted to discipline her. Strange. She is described here as a slave."

Gerrit blanched. Slaves were treated without mercy. Male or female alike, any slave that raised his or her hand, though without weapons, against master or mistress was summarily condemned to death. Impalement, breaking of limbs on a wheel and slow strangulation were among the methods of execution.

"Perhaps you had better attend the case yourself." Gysbert van Hoorn murmured quietly. De Goede hastened to the courtroom in a state of great shock. He scarcely recognised Helena Bas standing among those awaiting trial so changed was her appearance. Gone was what little composure she had when he last saw her. Her clothes were tattered and dirty. She averted her eyes when he looked at her. He hurried to the table of the prosecutor, Johan Keet, whom he knew. Weathering the stern gaze of the Landdrost who was about to hear the first case, he told Keet in an undertone that the defendant was in fact a freed slave and that he and the chief clerk to the Council of Policy had personally witnessed the document that confirmed this. He quickly outlined the circumstances. The Landdrost cleared his throat and de Goede returned to the back of the court.

"Is she a slave?" This was the Landdrost's first question when Helena was called to the dock. He appeared disinterested in the extreme. His eye flicked over the girl who was standing in front of the table in leg irons.

She was guarded by two soldiers.

"No sir. I have just learned that she was a slave in the employ of an officer of the Company, but has been given the status of a freed person, provided she returned to her land of origin which is Mauritius," the young prosecutor answered briskly.

"Why was I given to understand that she was a slave?"

"Apparently she did not reveal her true status. She wished to avoid deportation."

"What is she still doing here in the Cape?"

"Jumped ship, sir. She was a Company passenger on the *Postlooper* and she left the vessel without authority. The *Postlooper* has since sailed."

"May I say something, Sir?" Gerrit called out from the back of the courtroom. He could not contain himself even though he knew her was breaking a fundamental rule of the court.

"Who is that? Bring him in front of me," the Landdrost snapped. One of the soldiers took half a dozen strides, roughly pushing his way into the group of onlookers. He grabbed de Goede by the shoulder and dragged him to the front.

"What is your name?" the Landdrost enquired in a voice of quiet fury.

"De Goede, sir."

"Are you an officer of the court?"

"No sir. I am an officer of the Company. Junior clerk in the office of the Secretary to the Council of Policy."

"And what is your interest in this person?"

Gerrit explained that the first and only time he had seen Helena Bas was on board the *Postlooper*. "But I am afraid that this girl will make no effort to answer the charge. She appears to be in a state of extreme fright. Yet she has worked for many years in the home of a respectable official of the Company. She is thoroughly conversant in Dutch, but has probably concealed the fact for fear of detection."

"I will want to know in due course from burgher van Nierop the circumstances under which he acquired a slave who is not a slave. In the meantime, there is the question of punishment for desertion."

While the Landdrost was shuffling his papers, de Goede whispered to

Johan Keet. "What is this punishment likely to be?"

"The Landdrost is not in good feeling this day. He is likely to sentence her to be tethered to a post with an ox-hide over her head, to be scourged, branded and then banished from the Cape for ever."

Gerrit went pale and clutched his head. "He cannot do that. Helena is a civilised person. You must give me time to prevent this."

The prosecutor shook his head: "There is nothing I can do."

Gerrit de Goede had a dreadful aversion to physical punishment. He had to think of something to avoid the scourge. He was desperate. Then he remembered something that could prevent the sentence. The previous week he had read a letter from the Directors of the Company. This had been delivered in person by a Moravian missionary who came from Germany to attempt to convert the Hottentots to Christianity. The Assembly of Seventeen in Amsterdam resolved that a free passage to the Cape should be granted to him and advised the Council of Policy accordingly. The Directors required the Council to afford him such assistance as he might need.

"Mynheer, may I bring a matter of relevance to this case to the court's attention?"

The Landdrost glared at de Goede. "I have the impression that you are dangerously close to interfering in the execution of justice."

"No sir, with the utmost respect. A certain person with the name of Andries Schultz arrived at the Cape last month in the ship *Huis te Rensburg* with the object of converting Hottentots to Christianity. His mission to the Cape has been authorised by the Directors so that he might be blessed as an instrument for the conversion of ignorant and barbarous heathen, or at least for bringing them to a more moral and better mode of living."

"What did you say this man's name is? Andries Schultz? His presence here has already been observed. It is our information that he has taken to calling at the slave quarters notwithstanding the decree which strictly forbids anyone visiting these premises by day or night."

"That is indeed his name, Mynheer. But he is genuinely a missionary. The Reverend Andries Schultz is a widower from Germany who after a lifetime of hard work joined the Moravian mission after the death of wife. He volunteered to come to Africa to save the soul of the heathen."

"Is he of the Dutch Reformed Church?" The Company had a very close relationship with the official church of Holland. It was ordained, for instance that anyone absent from daily prayers should forfeit six days drink ration, while anyone absenting himself three times from daily prayer should do forced labour in chains at the public works for a year.

"No, Mynheer. Moravian." The Landdrost glowered. The Moravian mission was not officially recognized by the company and was viewed with some suspicion by the Dutch High Church Minister. De Goede hastened to add, "But the Directors specifically state that any converts must be presented to the clergyman of the parish for baptism to avoid a separate congregation being formed with rules differing from those of the Dutch Reformed Church. And the Reverend Schultz is fully conversant in Dutch, having a Dutch mother."

"What has this missionary got to do with the case before the court?"

"Mynheer, the missionary requires the services of an assistant who can interpret from the Hottentot's tongue. The accused will adequately fulfil this purpose. If the court allows a brief adjournment, I will summon the missionary to appear before Mynheer in person."

The Reverend Schultz, when he arrived at the court, glanced at Helena Bas. Gerrit de Goede had briefly explained the situation. "Well," the Landdrost said. "I am given to understand you are setting up a mission for the Hottentots here."

"Yes, Mynheer. I am a simple man of the cloth. I have come to this land to work with such people.

The Landdrost turned to the prosecutor and asked in a low voice: "He purports to be a man of God?"

"Yes sir. But as Mynheer has already remarked, his forays to the slave quarters have been observed."

"Is there any doubt in your mind as to the purpose of such visits?"

"It is not for me to surmise. Mynheer could always give him the *strappado*." This was the punishment meted out for the continued observance of such a practice, to ride the wooden horse for two days with a 12 lb weight on each leg. Men have been crippled thereby.

The Moravian missionary cleared his throat. "Mynheer, let me stand surety for the woman. She is not an evil person, I can see that. Release the young woman into my custody, sir."

"Do you understand that she has been charged with a serious offence, that of assault of a free burgher, and that by a slave?"

"Sir, I understand that respect for the rights of others is called justice. And that every violation of a right is an injustice."

"So, you are not arguing for her innocence in this case?"

"I am in no position to argue, only to ask."

"And what is your question?"

"What are the rights of a free burgher over a slave?"

"Is this a serious question?"

"Sir, we are speaking of justice. The greatest of all injustices, because it comprises all others, is slavery."

"How so, may I ask?"

"I owe respect to your liberty, sir. I owe respect to your body inasmuch as it belongs to you. I owe respect to your goods. But slavery is the subjecting of liberty, body and goods to the profit of another man. The only right left to the dreadful condition of slavery is the terrible right of insurrection against an odious power, the last resort of the oppressed against the abuse of force."

The face of the Landdrost darkened at these words. "You are preaching a dangerous doctrine. I could have you imprisoned for these views."

"Please do not misunderstand me. I am arguing from a philosophical point of view."

"I am not here in a philosophical capacity. I am here to uphold the law. We are discussing a legal system of duties that are provided by a person who is not fit for the level of full citizenship. Slaves, who have plenty of bodily strength for hard work, are intellectually of a lower order. Hence, they play a useful part in our society. Enough of this. I am too busy to debate this matter with a clergyman."

"Yes, sir. My wish is to establish a mission station at Baviaans' Kloof for these hapless people. The word of God is absent from their lives. They know not their own fathers sometimes."

"Aye. That is true. You would have to go far to find any other people so corrupt and devious. All right. I will agree to your request. This is an exercise in charity which is not obligatory. For justice, the formula is clear --- to respect the law. But charity knows neither rule nor limit."

"Well said, Mynheer," murmured the prosecutor who was wondering how his superior would extricate himself from this argument.

"You will be held personally responsible for her remaining in a fit state of employment. She must not become a burden on the Company," the Landdrost declared.

"Thank you, sir. We are obliged to seek a livelihood where we can and that is God's will. We have little of material possessions and we trust to their Lord to provide us with comfort and sustenance."

While these proceedings were underway, Gerrit de Goede watched Helena Bas. His relief seemed to be matched by hers. Her fear appeared to have subsided and she was no longer so tense. He was determined to see her again as soon as possible.

It was not until three months later, however, that he contrived a trip to Stellenbosch, the closest settlement to Baviaans' Kloof. Here the handsome Drostdy building surrounded by oak trees was situated on the banks of the river. Burghers grew large quantities of wheat in the fertile soils of the valley and vines were already well established on the mountain slopes. He rode out northwards the next day and came upon the mission. The pace of life there seemed leisurely. There were a number of Hottentot families who were accommodated in the environs. The Reverend Andries Schultz welcomed Gerrit. However he appeared to have changed in the short while since he had been there. His demeanour had become noticeably more messianic. His hair, always grey and unkempt, had grown wilder. His eyes flashed with zeal.

"How is your mission going?" De Goede enquired. He was desperate to see Helena but was obliged to observe the necessary civilities.

"They are very difficult to instruct in Christian principles and are not sufficiently far advanced in orderly living. Moreover many of the burghers here are strongly opposed to my work with the Hottentots. I have to cope with a great deal of popular prejudice. People believe that Moravians are fanatics and hold wild views of Christianity."

"Have any of your flock been baptised?" Gerrit asked, mindful of the restriction laid down by the company. "No. But I believe it is absurd that I should teach the Hottentots and then send them for baptism to ministers who have made no efforts for their conversion."

"And how is Helena Bas?" The reverend smiled warmly and Gerrit felt a cold hand on his heart. "I will call her. Helena, come and greet our visitor."

Helena Bas entered the room. Gerrit saw with a sickening finality that her belly was rounded with child. He looked in consternation at the Reverend Schultz. "May I ask you what your intentions are?"

"My doctrine, sir, is that all men are alike in the eyes of God. It is my Christian duty to this woman that I should marry her without regard to the colour of her skin."

"Marry her?" Gerrit echoed. "You who are old enough to be her father."

"True. And you might say she is not of my station. But I might have corrupted myself by marrying a woman of substance. Instead, by the grace of

God, my choice has been fixed on this young black girl whose only possessions are two sheepskins and a string of beads."

"Do you have her consent?" Gerrit's words rushed from his mouth without thought. He turned to Helena and took her hand. "What is your feeling? This old man wants to take you as his wife. What is your feeling to that?" While he watched her face with anguish in his eyes, the girl slipped her hand free from his grasp and ran to the older man and embraced him.

Gerrit stumbled out of the room. He hardly remembered returning to the settlement at Stellenbosch. He felt sick and disillusioned. He rebelled against the coarseness and brutality of life in the Cape yet he was unwilling to return to Holland. He believed his future lay in Africa. But what was he to do?

The Foundling

Nxi broke the back of the snake with a deft flick of his horny toes. It writhed in the sand for several seconds as Nxi watched with his bright black eyes. When the reptile was still, Nxi held it carefully at the neck, and with a blade of sharpened bone, delicately slit the upper jaw to expose the poison glands. He cut out these little sacs of colourless fluid on to a fragment of egg shell then let go the body of the snake. One of the Khoi women recovered it from the sand and thrust it into a skin bag.

Nxi was the head of one of a few families of Bushmen living in the uncompromising desert. His uncanny ability to survive in a hostile environment was not in any way diminished over the centuries in which his kinsfolk had been progressively driven to the most uninhabitable areas of the country. One of the most remarkable attributes of the Bushmen was their ability to make poison and was a secret they shared with no one.

Nxi had knowledge of a hidden grove of the particular bulb used for poison preparation. It was one with a fan-shaped leaf and a beautiful purple flower. Nxi selected the finest bulb and cleaned it of earth. He carefully sliced off its root ends. The silky-looking outer skins were peeled off and were themselves used as the receptacle for the creamy liquid which oozed from the bulb. When the flow ceased, a slice was cut from the lower end and the process repeated until the bulb was completely cut up. The liquid was then transferred into a gourd which was placed on a fire. Then he produced the snake venom which he had selected for the poison mixture --- these differed in terms of individual recipes --- and the tiny poison sacs were placed in the gourd.

Nxi noticed the faint blue wisp of smoke from the burning huts at the Capemen's discarded settlement. He changed direction slightly, and resumed his easy trot. He arrived at the camp, reduced now to a smouldering heap of ashes. His practised eye traversed the bush around the perimeter of the camp. He noticed, a few hundred yards from smoking ruin, a bundle under a bush.

He squatted on his haunches in characteristic pose and watched for some time before he ventured nearer. He discovered that it was a child and that the little creature was still alive, but only just. He was suspicious. The Capemen who lived in the settlement were as likely as not trying to trap him. He had spent many hours watching them from his lookout point on a sand dune, unobserved as he blended into the surroundings. They guarded their cattle closely and drove them into an enclosure at night. The Khoi would occasionally steal a beast when it strayed from the others in the late afternoon. But it was risky.

While Nxi was watching the child and considering the proximity of the Capemen who must have left their settlement earlier that day, he heard the soft greeting of his wife, Tlepi. Nxi summoned her to his side to observe the small bundle of life under the bush with not much chance of survival.

"We leave it. It is not of ours," Nxi grunted. But he knew Tlepi would decide herself. She wrapped the infant in a scrap of animal skin and carried back to the Khoi encampment where the rest of the tribe were waiting. They sat under several rough shelters of antelope hides held up by sticks, inconspicuous in the hollow of the sand, and capable of being quickly taken down for portage to the next stage.

Nxi and Tlepi laid their charge carefully in the shade. Tlepi's mother, now that she was an old woman and no longer an active member of the little community, was known as Ma-tlepi, uncovered her collection of herbs. She set to work to revive the girl. She propped up the little head, and allowed a few drops of evil-smelling water from an ostrich egg to run into its mouth. She applied fat to the fair skin horribly burned by the sun and a vegetable oil to the pained eyes, all the while crooning a gentle lullaby.

The next morning, the little band of Bushmen set out across the desert, taking a northerly direction. Nxi ranged ahead of the others, always alert and on the lookout for danger --- or for food. At night they slept beneath their crude shelters, Ma-tlepi cuddling the pale infant close to her wasted body. It was two days before they reached their secret waterhole. It was situated in a dry river bed, and the presence of water was not in any way apparent to an outsider.

Ma-tlepi was the nominated woman who dug down at the appointed place, removing the sand which showed just the faintest trace of water. She filled the cavity with dry grass, first shoving a hollow reed into the wet sand.

Then, with infinite patience, and taking occasional turns with the other woman, she sucked up the water as the sand at the bottom of the hole became saturated. The precious liquid was dribbled out of her mouth, running down a straw into an ostrich egg. This procedure continued for many hours until no less than 30 eggs had been filled. Ten of these were distributed among the tribe for portage. Those not required for the journey were carried carefully in a skin bag to a hiding place several miles away, and buried for later use.

The little girl was given a generous ration of water under the circumstances, and Ma-tlepi took the opportunity to bathe her body of the grit and dust which aggravated her healing skin. In doing this she had to stare down the hostile glances of the others. Their resentment at the apparent wastage of this precious commodity was not disguised.

Over the next six moons Ma-tlepi protected the little girl as far as possible from the extreme discomfort and hardship they experienced every day. Relieved of some of her chores she would collect morsels of gum from a particular type of acacia and coax the child to chew upon it.

She would also forego her share of any birds eggs that were distributed, or the tasty moramma beans, wild cucumbers, grass seeds, berries, bulbs and tubers that the tribe was able to consume at various stages, bringing a richness and variety to their otherwise sparse diet. Exotic dishes there were too. Ants' eggs --- called bushmen's rice --- together with the ants themselves with their broad black heads and long flat bodies.

Nevertheless, as the long months went by, no one really got enough food. Summer was almost over and yet no rain had fallen. The air was dry, the hot sun relentless. Shade could nowhere be found and in the afternoons, the strong winds whipped stinging grains of sand against their bodies as they staggered on.

A marauding band of hyenas began to follow their progress through the desert. Nxi stoked up the fire before they went to sleep. But in the darkness, when the fire had died down, one fearless hyena approached their encampment.

Ma-tlepi was instantly awake as the animal tugged at the skin blanket which she and the child shared. She shouted and waved her hand in a gesture of helpless defiance as the sleeping child was dragged away. The hyena left the blanket and snapped at Ma-tlepi's arm inflicting a terrible gash. The screams of the old woman, and the child who had now awoken in terror aroused the others and in the ensuing uproar the hyena slunk away.

It was soon after they reached the outlying grassy plains of the delta, their destination for the winter months, that Ma-tlepi took ill. Not only had the strain of caring for the child over the past six or more months taken its toll. But the poisonous bite of the hyena refused to heal properly. She realised her time had come. No bushman family could afford to have old and infirm people kept on indefinitely. They would only be a drain on the resources and mobility of the fit members.

Ma-tlepi was given a twist of dagga and left in a spot sheltered from the sun and wind. Nxi returned a few moments later leading the white girl by the hand. He motioned her to stay with the old woman and departed.

Ma-tlepi pressed her eyes closed, her whole face becoming a mass of tiny wrinkles. Her peppercorn hair was sparse, her gums toothless. Yet she summoned her strength and after chewing determinedly on the dagga, staggered to her feet. She took the child by the hand and together they made their slow progress towards the low hills in the distance. It was another full day and night --- spent in the crutch of a thorn tree to avoid predators --- before the pair arrived at the furthermost kraal of the permanent black community.

The white girl was handed over to one of the women tilling the ground on the outskirts of the kraal. Ma-tlepi then sat down and within a few minutes she had expired.

Motsumi the Hunter

Motsumi had a happy childhood. His earliest memories were of a hollow tree within which his body fitted comfortably and where he could dream happily, within call of help if he got frightened or lonely. He was kept in the company of the old women during the day while his mother, Bontle , joined the other young mothers working in the fields, tilling maize, pumpkin and millet. After work, Bontle gathered *morok*, the wild spinach that was such a favourite of her husband, Matisane. She mixed the morok with putu, stiff maize porridge, which made it more palatable. Matisane always ate by himself and his portion of putu was often mixed with chillies which were far too hot for Motsumi.

During the long days Motsumi played with the other children. They collected bird's eggs, lay in the grass and imitated the calls of animals. They became thoroughly familiar with the ways of the bush. One morning Motsumi was playing at home among some loose stones when a scorpion, quite fascinating with tail curled back over its body, emerged from beneath a stone. The little boy reached out to grasp it and recoiled in agony when, with a strange sizzling sound, it flung itself at him and attached its sting to his arm before scuttling away.

Bontle, who chanced to be working in a field within hearing distance, dropped her hoe when she heard the little boy's shrieks and hastened back to the hut. She realised at once what had happened. Without pausing to comfort the child, she began turning over the stones, one after the other, until she found what she wanted, another scorpion. Then Bontle picked up her screaming boy and carried him to the spot where the scorpion was crouched, its stinging tail describing a low arc across its back. Bontle held out the boy's arm, despite his frantic struggling. Relentlessly she offered it to the scorpion. Motsumi went almost out of his mind in terror, his little body already throbbing with pain and nausea from the first sting, and his whole being rebelling against any repetition of this dreadful and agonising experience. But his mother was firm. The scorpion, confused by the shrieks of the child, held back. But Bontle brushed Motsumi's arm against the reptile until the inevitable occurred. The little creature reared up and the angry red dart of its sting entered the soft flesh of the arm, adjacent to the earlier wound.

Motsumi fainted with the pain. Bontle took him back to her hut, soothing him with soft crooning and stroking him softly. This was the only antidote she knew --- a second sting to be administered within minutes of the first. Incredibly, before an hour was passed, Motsumi was once more running and playing with the other children.

It was summer and after the rain Bontle sent the children off to collect mopane worms, the caterpillars of the large brown moth which bore a striking array of colours in the form of a fierce face mask on the back to repel its predators. Mopane worms were a delicacy in the district and they represented a valuable protein addition to the people's diet. Bontle roasted and then dried these tasty caterpillars and stored them for months in a small skin bag hidden in the roof of her hut. In the winter, when other food was scarce, she carefully reconstituted these fragile light husks with water and the family ate them with stiff porridge.

She would take Motsumi with her to the mopane woods half a day's walk from the kraal. The trees with their distinctive butterfly like leaves grew closely together. During the heat of the day the leaves hung straight down like ribbons, thus causing very little shade. Yet from any distance, the foliage appeared dense. It also concealed from all but Motsumi's sharp eyes any animals that might be standing, quietly panting in the heat, in a strange muted sunlight. Matisane told his son that he never hunted antelope which had been browsing in mopane trees. The leaves had a strong aromatic smell which imparted a taint to the meat. Mopane wood was valuable, almost black in colour, durable, hard and heavy. It was an excellent medium for carving and the effort of carrying a sturdy mopane branch back to the local woodcarvers earned Motsumi a small reward. Even the chips were saved for the fire. When burnt, they gave off a sweet smell and an intense heat.

Matisane showed his son a nest of black soldier ants. These represented the highest degree of unity and organisation to be found in nature. They could well nigh cover the entire body of an animal or man with so light a tread as to betray no indication of their presence. Not until each ant was in position to attack will any straggler so far controvert discipline as to snatch a meal for himself in anticipation of orders. But when the psychological moment had arrived, some signal was arranged or sounded in a note too insignificant to strike the senses of the giant he attacked and precisely at that moment hundreds of small forceps tear away as many minute morsels of meat until, in the case of a tethered calf, a chained dog, a cooped fowl or a man tied down by the fiendish ingenuity of his fellows, the victim is by small degrees deprived of flesh and life.

When his son was a little older, Matisane and Motsumi spent many days in the bush. Matisane's favourite spot was a nearby river where, in the summer months the water would back up for a great distance and this became a haven for the game. With Matisane's gentle encouragement and help, Motsumi developed a remarkable ability to understand the ways of wild animals. His father promised to make him a bow and arrows if he could catch the calf of a sitatunga, the shyest and least known of all African fauna. Its very rarity made it a sought-after prey and Matisane said he would let his son present the antelope to the chief who would be sure to honour the child.

So, one morning just at first light, Motsumi made his way to the river determined to stalk this timid antelope on his own. He spent nearly the whole day watching it in a patch of reeds in the water before a young sitatunga appeared, invisible to all but the eye of the young hunter. For another hour he watched it moving noiselessly among the reeds sometimes submerging entirely when feeding. He slid into the water downstream from the reeds and very carefully started to approach. He knew that if he was careless enough to snap a twig with his foot or move a branch, or at the slightest sign of danger sensed only by the small animal, it would hide under the water, with only its nose showing. And then it would creep away into the thicker undergrowth and disappear.

So Motsumi waded very cautiously and quietly into the shallows, going from one antheap to another. He would have to merge himself completely into the surroundings if he was to come upon the sitatunga in stealth. It took a great deal of practice to become adept at stalking in water. He kept his feet more or less flat on the bottom and moved forward in a shuffling manner. He encountered a heavy object with his toes and realised with heart-stopping horror that he had slid his foot under a small crocodile. But he was fortunate to find that the reptile was not aggressive and it slid silently away along the river bed. A frightened crocodile might have lashed out with its tail with disastrous consequences. The only other danger that he dreaded was the presence of a lion taking refuge on an anthill in the shade of the reeds and waiting himself for an unwary sitatunga to approach.

However, what happened then was of far greater danger than he could have foreseen. An organised hunting party of neighbouring tribesmen had moved into the area to search out sitatunga with fire. The leader set alight the dry papyrus above the water line and the blaze soon took hold. Fanned by the wind, the fire swept through the huge grove of reeds, driving before it myriads of birds and insects. Waterfowl flew out in front of the flames and even the crocodiles and hippos thrashed about in the shallows.

The spearmen lined up along the water's edge in readiness for the fleeing game, the sitatunga always being the prize. Motsumi, who was desperately trying to quell the panic that throbbed in his breast, knew that his only salvation lay in adopting the same strategy as the shy quarry and submerging himself until the searing heat and crackling flames had passed by. He gripped a reed in his mouth and slowly drew in enough air to keep his lungs filled. But another strategy was brought into play by the hunters. The intrepid men entered their makoros --- hollowed tree trunks --- and punted slowly into the smoking and matted reed beds, seeking out any antelope that still remained. The leading spearman knelt on the prow watching for movement in the water. The man navigating the craft changed direction in response to indications from the leader as he searched for tell-tale lines of bubbles.

Motsumi was not to realise the dreadful proximity of a sitatunga until almost too late. In one instant he sensed the imminence of the *makoro* parting the reeds to one side of him, and almost simultaneously a nervous movement next to him betrayed the presence of the animal to the hunter. The man immediately plunged his spear downward with great force. There was a horrible commotion underwater, and Motsumi tasted rather than saw the sudden discolouration as clouds of dark blood swirled about. The animal, still thrashing in agony, was lifted onto the *makoro* and its death hastened by a blade drawn across its throat. The hunters cheered and turned for the shore, leaving the boy cowering in the water.

It was only when he straightened up in the shallows that he noticed the situtunga's calf lying motionless on a rough raft of reeds bent down to form a nest just above the water line. Its mother had been crouching in the water only a few yards ahead and Motsumi realised the tremendous power of maternal love, far stronger than that of self-survival. He took the little creature and waded carefully away. He told his father that the sitatunga's mother had been taken by a hunting party before he could do anything but that he had stalked and captured the calf entirely on his own. Matisane was very proud of his son and presented the little antelope to the chief. He duly presented Matisane with his first set of arrows and a bow.

From that moment on, Motsumi practised every day until he was as proficient as any of the hunters in the tribe, a talent that he combined with quite exceptional bravery. His first major success was in shooting a lion which had attacked the goats in the kraal. When the lion was discovered early one morning by the women going out to till the maize lands, it was Motsumi who quickly appeared. With his weapon at the ready, he positioned himself near the entrance, and sinking down on one knee, he unleashed an arrow into the lion's shoulder at short range. The animal roared with pain and fury but when it tried to rush at its young adversary, its forefoot crumpled underneath as a result of the wound in its shoulder. While it was struggling on its side, the young hunter drove two more arrows into its chest, one entering the heart and causing instant death.

Motsumi was praised by the tribal elders and received the skin of the lion as his trophy. What was more valuable to the young lad was the tacit approval by the elders to his spending all of his time roaming the bush with his bow and arrow.

As his strength developed and his stature grew into that of a man, Motsumi fashioned himself bows of greater size, with the gut bowstring being cut from the intestines of a giraffe. The arrows fitted with vulture feathers could thereby be sent away with unprecedented velocity. He also began experimenting with vegetable poisons to improve the effectiveness of his hunting. It was on his fifteenth year that he achieved a distinction that was to change the course of history for the tribe. He shot and killed a fully-grown elephant bull which was quietly feeding in the tall rushes down at the river, and was heading steadily towards the mealie crops that were due for harvesting within the week. Saba used the same technique of shooting through the shoulder just missing the central comb of the scapula, and penetrating the lung. The arrow ripped through the hardened muscle of the shoulder, and the elephant immediately whirled away from the pain. It made for the tall trees upriver, its progress hindered by the rapidly laming leg, and *acacanthra* poison from the arrow spreading its paralysis.

Meanwhile the lesion in the lung had caused a flooding of lymph and blood into the chest, and the great beast found it increasingly difficult to breathe. But it continued doggedly on its course, and for three agonising miles it blundered on. Finally it came to a standstill under a grove of marula trees, probing with the tip of its trunk the wound on its shoulder, the arrow shaft having long since been brushed off. But the poison had entered the central nervous system and the elephant was unable to proceed any further.

Motsumi squatted patiently on his haunches a mere hundred yards away. He knew he had won. Now it was just a question of waiting for the final moment that he could walk up to the elephant and observe its death when with a groan it would sink on its chest, its head supported by its tusks, and with its own weight squeezing the last of the air out of its lungs, it would die of suffocation.

At the end of the second day, with the whole village watching the final agony, the elephant expired exactly as Motsumi had predicted. It was the first time that an elephant had been killed with an arrow in that area, and Motsumi's reputation was established throughout the region.

Giraffe skin was a sought after material for ceremonial clothing. The skin cut from the neck was particularly favoured, not for the colour since after decomposition set in, all the hair fell out. Rather it was for is consistency. The skin, after being stretched out in the sun to dry for several days, would be moistened again by the saliva of the women, then rubbed, twisted, pulled and trampled until it became as pliable as cloth and as white as the plumage of the egret.

On the annual giraffe hunt, which was something of a ceremony, the chief's son was appointed to be the leading spearman. Motsumi had to accept this imposition although he feared the young man was inexperienced and likely to be a danger. Accordingly, after Motsumi brought the giraffe down with an arrow, the chief's son was given the task of making the kill. The giraffe was still mobile and stumbled to its feet again. It could not move properly because of the lameness of its back leg. The chief's son was able to run alongside it for a few paces while it staggered along and plunge his spear in the rib cage. But it did not find its mark and only served to slow the animal down further. Another spear was driven into the animal, but again without finesse. Finally, the beast turned to face its pursuer and began pawing the earth, its long neck bent almost to the ground and swaying to and fro. Motsumi called out to the

young man in anger. "Give me your short spear. I will show you what to do."
He walked calmly up to the animal. But as if to reassert its pride, the giraffe,
marking the approach of the man, swung its neck sideways like a giant snake
and then, whirling it through the air in a vicious arc, it hit the human with
a bone-shattering thud, propelling Motsumi's body high into the air, and
joining its foe in death.

While this awful finale was being played out, several other giraffe were
observing the scene, looking timidly from their eyries in the tree tops like
children peeping from behind the curtains of an upstairs window.

Vater Friedrich

Yes, with his burning blue eyes and prematurely grey hair, the young missionary seemed to Chief Makotla to be possessed of magical powers. Friedrich joined the Berlin Missionary Society aged 25, and elected to travel to the furthermost parts of southern Africa to "conquer for Christ." After journeying northwards from the Cape along the "missionary road," he needed a short while to recover from his journey before proceeding further into the desert to "uproot heathen beliefs and instil Christian ideals and Christian life." It was while he was staying temporarily at a remote trading post that Chief Makotla heard of his presence. He sent an emissary to the place with a gift of two oxen for the chief of the area in which the trading store was situated. Having obtained permission from the chief, the emissary begged an audience with Friedrich. Through an interpreter, he requested the missionary to make his home with the Barutsi people. He would lead them there. The devout German believed this was indeed a signal from the Lord. Preceded by a scout, the emissary and twenty men struck out westward through the desert until they reached a wonderful oasis alongside the banks of a broad, slow-flowing river. They were welcomed by chief Mokatla, traditional head of the Barutsi tribe.

The Chief had heard of missionaries. They were the medicine men of the Europeans. This newcomer must possess knowledge of medicine exceedingly more powerful than his own medicine men. Surely, such a man would be able to prevent the terrible destruction being wreaked on the Barutsi people in these troublesome times. He was told that it was only through the efforts of the missionaries of the London Society that the dreaded conqueror Moselikatse had ceased his terrible deprivations over the weaker tribes in the area. The missionaries must have been able to exert a mighty influence over the warrior chief. Makotla concluded that the missionaries could only have obtained such influence by magic. He became most eager to obtain a missionary who would impart such valuable knowledge to him.

"You are welcome," Chief Makotla told his visitor through an interpreter. "I see you. I am pleased you are safely here." Miraculously they had not been molested along the way. Makotla's own medicine man said that this was because he had fumigated the chief with the smoke of a certain root to "open the way" for them. Whatever the cause, the white visitor was lucky for the conditions of the territory were chaotic. The peace-loving Barutsi people had been scattered by the invaders from the east and most of their cattle had been driven off. They had lost all their fighting men in the encounter and were only saved by their own flight into the desert. They had returned later to rebuild their burnt homes and mourn their dead. Throughout the region, entire tribes were wandering about without cattle, homes or food. They were attacked again and again. They eked out a miserable existence. Order was difficult to establish. Chief Makotla was among the luckier ones.

Vater Friedrich, surveying the chief and his elders seated under a huge tree on the edge of the desert, said he too was pleased. Secretly he was quite amazed that his reception was so cordial. He was immediately fired with added zeal in bringing light to these children. "I bring you the Word of God," he told his uncomprehending audience. He was soon to realise, however, that he was expected to teach the chief the secret arts which made the white men so rich and so powerful. Makotla was quite convinced that this could be done through potent charms and medicines. For Friedrich, this was the start of an arduous, frustrating and heart-breaking period. In his seemingly hopeless task of instructing the people in the way of God, he was to learn with dreadful despondency that the black tribes were not easily changed from their traditional ways. They were most reluctant to abandon their belief in ancestor gods for a belief in Christ. Only very occasionally were Friedrich's efforts at "converting the heathen" rewarded with success. And then the subject quite often reverted. It required all the German characteristics of doggedness and determination to keep his morale.

And it was Aribaa-nyana, who had come to work for the mission as a young girl, who tried to help him to understand the tribal myths, as he called them, and how to cope with a seemingly intransigent chief. Riba, as he called her, was an exceptionally bright girl and he taught her to speak German so that she could be his interpreter. Riba, being a practical female, looked at things in a different way to him. She recognised his frustrations in trying to get the people to appreciate the Good Word. She also realised he was going about things in entirely the wrong way. From the start, she begged Vater Friedrich to let her introduce him to her mother so that they could discuss matters of importance. Surely he could appreciate that these women wielded one of the greatest influences in the tribe? It was only after constant persuasion that he was finally taken to Aribaa, the rainmaker. It was an auspicious occasion when he was taken to the home of she who presided over the annual rainmaking ceremonies at the chief's kraal, when an ox would be slaughtered and placed in a large pool in the river. This was a powerful supplication to the gods, and not entirely unwelcome to the crocodiles, Vater Friedrich said to himself.

The missionary at last heard that it was Riba's mother who had been brought up in the household of chief Makotla. "Yes," the interpreter explained. "I was conceived after Chief Makotla himself honoured my mother with his attention."

Riba told the reverend father that her mother's position in the tribe, although a senior one, was not secure. At any moment Chief Mokatla could banish her or order her to be thrown into the crocodile pool. Vater Friedrich was soon able to hold discussions with the chief and his elders and began to acquire an understanding of tribal religion, the outstanding feature of which was a worship of spirits as distinct from God. The abodes of these spirits were mainly the tribal ancestors but they also ranged from the forces of nature to trees and animals. The people feared mightily that their ancestors, unless regularly appeased by worship and by sacrifice, would become angry and wreak revenge. Any calamity that befell the tribe was due to the displeasure of the spirits. And it was natural then that a class of people emerged who claimed the power of discovering what displeased the ancestral spirits. Soon, however, it became easier for the "diviner" to "smell out" a tribesman or woman who was casting evil spells that caused the illness of the chief, for example, or the failure of crops. The person thus named would be subjected to excruciating torments, even death. His possessions would become the property of the chief and the diviner.

Vater Friedrich learnt that the three great commandments taught to every child were to honour your elders, worship your chief and sacrifice to your ancestral spirits. The children were quick to understand that when their forefathers died, they were never wholly dead. They survived as spirits. Thus the will of the people was perpetuated. The tribal law was sustained by their ancestors. The present chief was the male descendant of the spirit chiefs. And on regular occasions, sacrifices were made to appease the spirits or invoke their help.

Friedrich, in the end, refused to accept the validity of the tribal beliefs. He came to the reluctant conclusion that his faith was being distorted by continued contact with Aribaa. It was hurtful to both her and her daughter when he no longer sought the company of the rain-maker. But Vater Friedrich now decided to concentrate his greatest efforts on the children. He appealed to the chief for permission to start a school. He offered to provide a daily meal to any of the tribal children who agreed to attend instruction. The young would surely be susceptible to the teaching of the Word, if he could get them early enough. But the children lived a carefree life. The boys, as soon as they could walk, were assigned to the herding of kids. Later, as they grew stronger, they were put in charge of calves and goats, and finally full cattle herds. Their early adolescence was spent in the veld where they studied the habits and characteristics of animals and birds. They acquired skill in hunting. The girls fetched water, stamped corn and acted as nursemaids for babies not much smaller than themselves. The children accepted unquestioning obedience to their elders as the ultimate fount of wisdom and experience. And Friedrich's offer of food attracted but a handful of children.

He suffered spells of black despair. He told himself that the magnitude of the task --- in which individual boys and girls would have to be convinced to forego the influence of their fathers, mothers and families to pursue their own salvation --- ensured its inevitable failure. Surely, he said to himself, the moral power was the will of the people. One cannot change that. The whole tribe was held together by that belief. Indeed it was their tribal solidarity that had saved Makotla's people from the invaders and their faith in their ancestral gods had not been shaken. Then Friedrich's faith would return. "The Word of the Lord is like a beacon of light," he said. He spoke aloud to reassure himself.

"I am convinced that boys, under the influence of Christian teaching, will be persuaded to stay away from the initiation schools. I have heard how they dread these ordeals when they are subjected to starvation and blows, discomfort and actual torture, when they are made to undertake strenuous hunting expeditions and when the unruly boys are treated with especial ferocity." But all the same, he knew that any boys who did attend his classes and stayed away from the tribal initiation would be shunned by the rest of the tribe. The girls would refuse to have anything to do with them.

"If only, Oh Lord, I could make but a single conversion to maintain my faith. Teach me to have more understanding of these simple people. Their religion is so different to ours. They believe in their own sky god, yes. But they do not worship him. They worship their blasted ancestors," he added irreverently.

Chief Makotla's witch doctors, predictably, would have nothing to do with the mission. After the chief's initial enthusiasm had been quenched, and they regained their influence over the chief, they lost no opportunity in pressing their advantage home. The white man is trying to entice your subjects away, they said. If any of your subjects became Christians, they said, they would owe their loyalty elsewhere. They would no longer pay homage to the ancestral gods. They persuaded a deputation of elder tribesmen to go to Chief Makotla and complain to him for giving away the best part of their land. They wanted the mission station to be moved to another part of the valley. Vater Friedrich was aware of this groundswell of resistance but he refused to be intimidated.

That year there was a particularly bad drought. The river dried up completely, and the people were unable to get sufficient drinking water, let alone keep their meagre crops alive. Vater Friedrich, despite himself, was in dread that his erstwhile friend, the rainmaker, would be held accountable for the weather. He tried to discredit the rainmaking process and invited the chief to visit the mission. He told the chief that he wanted to prove to the ignorant heathen that, with God's help he had built a stone house, dug a well, started an irrigation scheme and was already growing crops. "This will provide irrefutable evidence of the power of the great Lord and the wisdom of his Word." It would also discredit the traditional rainmaker, he added and enhance Christianity.

Chief Makotla arrived at the appointed time. With him were a group of his trusted elders and Aribaa. Friedrich greeted the party warmly. He rang a bell which was mounted on a pole. This was to be the start of his church, he told them. He tried to speak to them in terms that they would understand.

"Who can touch the stars with his hand? Who makes the wind blow? Who sends the clouds which come and go, melt into water in the earth? Who is the God of all people?" He rang the bell again.

Chief Makotla said: "Your God gave the white man his knowledge of guns.

Our God gave us his knowledge of rainmaking."

Vater Friedrich suppressed his anger. "Does your rainmaker bring the clouds? Does he have superior powers?"

The chief turned to Aribaa. "This is my rainmaker, Aribaa. Ask her."

Aribaa said: "When the sky becomes overcast, then the rain is in the chief's mouth."

"But what happens when there are no clouds?"

"The rainmaker must dig up the body of a young child that has died a year ago as an invocation to the spirits." Aribaa cast her head down when she spoke.

Friedrich went doggedly on. "If you are able to make rain, how do you do it, Aribaa?"

"I do not say so; I say I seek the rain."

"And when you seek it, do you find it? And bring it to this land?"

"I have often given rain to this country. Here is the Chief who knows that I have done so on many occasions."

"Well, now I think rain comes from God. Here is the Book (and he showed the New Testament) it says that God gives rain. 'He gave us rain from Heaven, and fruitful seasons, filling our hearts with food and gladness.'"

"The Book speaks truly. I also say that God gives the rain," Aribaa answered.

"How so? You said now that you have the rain, and you give rain."

"I have the rain. I ask rain from the spirits, and I would give it, but I am hindered."

"Well, Aribaa. This is strange. You have the rain and here is the whole countryside burning with the sun. The lands are parched. The river has stopped running. Your cattle are wasting away. If you have rain, why not give it without delay?"

There was a murmur of approval from some of the elders, and Aribaa looked angry and confused. "I would give the rain. I have been trying for three moons but there is something that turns the rain."

"Ha," Friedrich looked triumphantly at her, as though he had won a victory. "Why don't you tell us what is this hindrance?"

This time it was Aribaa's turn to look triumphant. "I have slaughtered cattle and offered sacrifices to the spirits. When the clouds come up and spread over the land and the rain is ready to fall, that thing you have brought into our land makes a noise and the clouds scatter. No rain can fall. You ask me? Then I will tell you. You are the hindrance."

The chief applauded vigorously. Aribaa turned away. The missionary stepped forward. "You accuse me, Vater Friedrich of stopping the rain from falling? Now I know that you speak lies." There was a sudden and ominous intake of breath from the chief and his elders. But he went on. "This bell calls people to worship, to worship God. Perhaps it is God who keeps the rain away from those people who believe in spirits and not in Him."

He called Aribaa to his side and then asked her if she thought God should be worshipped. She shook her head. "Then show this man the power you have," she was ordered. Vater Friedrich looked up at the cloudless sky and gave thanks to God. He believed that the Chief's prejudice against him and his mission would be significantly reduced if Aribaa could not perform his wish. But he was ignorant of the power of traditional belief.

Three days later the rainmaker, who was meant to inspire the whole tribe with her vigour and strength, called the chief and all the elders together to participate in a tribal rain hunt. She led the procession across the valley and as they passed by the villages, they were progressively joined by all the able-bodied men of the tribe. Aribaa went ahead into a grove of trees followed by the assembly. There they were to witness her final ceremony. She invoked the gods and then lay down in an open grave. With great dignity and composure, she gave the order for it to be filled in. A great cry arose from the people and Vater Friedrich and Riba clearly heard from the mission the ululations drifting over the valley. They both knew subconsciously that something terrible and final had happened. Riba sobbed uncontrollably and refused to be comforted by the distraught missionary.

Next morning the tribe woke to the sound of gently falling rain.

The Prince and the Hunt

Prince Alfred Ernest Albert, second son of Queen Victoria paid a visit to the Cape in July 1860[1]. It was the first occasion that a member of the Royal Family called on this part of the British dominion, and the prospect attracted the keen interest of the inhabitants, black and white alike.

The prince, who was then a midshipman on the steam frigate Euryalus, made a grand tour of the country. Jocelyn turned her mind to an officer of the regiment who had appeared to be attracted to her but to date had never received any encouragement to his attentions. He was mildly surprised when Jocelyn asked eagerly for details of the royal tour when they happened to meet outside the Drostdy Gate near the Fort. Captain Antrobus, neat and erect, twirled his moustache.

"Well, they arrive at Simon's Bay towards the end of the month. There will be a reception the next afternoon in Cape Town where, I am certain, every possible demonstration of welcome will be made by the officials and the troops at the Castle."

The Captain told of the further arrangement. "A short visit to Stellenbosch, the Paarl and Drakenstein will follow. There will be receptions at all these places which will show, if such proof is wanted, that the Dutch-speaking colonists can be as thoroughly loyal to Her Majesty the Queen as any people not of English descent could possibly be."

"And then, and then..." Jocelyn could hardly keep the impatience out of her voice. Why was this man so ponderous and stuffy?

"After this short tour of the oldest part of the Colony, the Prince will

1   Acknowledgement to The Life and Times of Sir George Grey, KCB by William Lee Rees, 1892

proceed by sea to Port Elizabeth. And can you guess? I have been assigned to his retinue for the overland journey from Algoa Bay all the way up to Port Natal. I believe I might even be accompanying him back on the Euryalus which will be waiting at the harbour there. I'm due to return home for long leave anyway and the commanding officer here thinks this can be arranged."

An official letter was delivered several days later. Captain Antrobus requested the pleasure of her company at a Ball at the Garrison to welcome His Royal Highness, the Prince of Wales. Her friends admired the invitation with the official coat of arms. "I cannot possibly go," she told them. But such an opportunity would not present itself again, they responded. After all, how often did a Royal Personage visit Grahams Town. But of course, she had already decided. She would accept. And what is more, she would somehow connive a passage to England for herself. And if her plan succeeded, then let the ensuing scandal take care of itself. She would not be here to bother about the whisperings of few so-called society ladies. Her mother did not really need her any more. And her half-brothers would understand.

Captain Antrobus was overjoyed when her reply was received. He looked forward to seeing her on her morning walk and saying how much he appreciated her kind acceptance. But he didn't have the chance as she changed her practice, or her route, and he did not set eyes on her before the time came for him to leave for Algoa Bay to meet the Prince.

An official record was published to mark the Royal Visit. Captain Antrobus was one of the correspondents. He described the Prince as "barely 16 years old but very dignified. When we arrived for escort duties, he was already waiting, dressed in what was described as South African hunting costume --- felt helmet hat, dark cloth jacket, cord trousers and top boots. There was a large troop of horsemen forming the Royal party and many hundreds of civilians mounted on their horses followed on behind, as well as carriages and carts of all descriptions."

At the Zwartkops River a huge array of children were gathered to wish the Prince farewell. Then came the wonderful ride. For three hours, the Prince and his hunting companions galloped across the Amsterdam Flats. "It was all fair South African coursing," Captain Antrobus wrote, "and the burst was glorious. Bucks and hares were quickly set afoot and the hounds showed how well they could conduct the sport .The Prince rode among the foremost in the chase and held his seat and reins as firmly as any Nimrod. The escort of men, with fat horses and heavy baggage, were soon left behind." The trip to Grahamstown took two days, with stops for meals and overnight accommodation at Settler villages en route. The welcome was everywhere most profuse. Arches were erected over the road on numerous points and people gathered to cheer and wave flags.

Jocelyn went to witness the *fete champetre* which was held on the outskirts of the town in honour of the Prince. The committee of citizens had worked diligently for several weeks and the results of their efforts were manifest in the shape of pavilions, tents, banners, arches and decorations of every sort, and the vast assemblage who were present to meet the royal visitor. Not least among the participants were members of the black community with improvised banners "uncouth in form and more loyal than artistic in device and general get-up," Captain Antrobus told Jocelyn. "These naturally provoked amongst the crowded people along the route loud peals of good-humoured laughter, in which the swarthy bannerers themselves joined most heartily."

On the night of the ball, the town was brilliantly illuminated, as were the Hottentot locations. The fort and Government House shone out with all the brightness which sperm and oil could furnish, gas unhappily was there still unknown --- while bonfires blazed with magnificent effect from all the hills around. Jocelyn and Captain William Antrobus walked hand in hand to the ball, the Captain having first dined with his fellow officers at Government House with the Prince. They waved as the Prince himself passed by in an open carriage drawn by a band of youths from the town preceded by a young sailor boy in nautical attire. The procession was illuminated by Chinese lamps carried by the sprightly boys.

It was a glittering affair with all the officers in their dress uniforms and the civilians in tails and wing collar shirts with black ties, the womenfolk in full-length gowns. The Prince charmed them all. His presence was quite dominant although his stature was surprisingly small.

Jocelyn danced with the Captain, waltzes, mazurkas and gavottes. She allowed him to be entranced by her. She rested her hand on his shoulder and occasionally ran her fingers lightly along his neck. And when it was time to say goodbye, she leaned up and kissed him on the lips. The Captain squeezed her tenderly, then more urgently. She withdrew and then kissed him with sudden passion.

"Now, that's that," she said with a playful smile. "We mustn't get too serious."

"Oh, but I am serious, my dear lady. I would do anything..." but she would not let him finish. She pressed a finger lightly on his lips.

"But hear me, please. Nothing would make me happier than to take you with me, away from here, to marry me. Would you, would you consent?"

"I cannot answer, I need time to think. Oh, but to get away from here. If only I could." If only, she continued to herself, the good captain did not take himself so seriously.

Captain Antrobus told Jocelyn that his father was very strict. "He taught me to ride a horse, to tell the truth, to love my country and to honour soldiers." Jocelyn thought her admirer behaved like a very responsible schoolboy. He liked to call his seniors "Sir." He stood for manly values. She was certain he took a cold bath every morning. The colonial empire needed men like him, plain English gentlemen, with an almost passionate conception of fair play, of protection of the weak and of playing the game.

The Captain left the next morning with the official party. His first letter arrived two weeks later, via the military bag.

"I have done nothing but think of you," he wrote. "Ever since I left your side, I can hardly pay attention to my duties for longing of you." He wrote about the tour. From Grahamstown they travelled eastwards through Fort Beaufort and Alice to King William's Town.

"Along this line there is in many places very good scenery and everywhere something of interest can be observed. It passes through the heart of the territory that for three quarters of a century has been the battleground of the white immigrants moving up from the west and the black immigrants moving down from the east, where no trace of the aboriginal inhabitants is left except their paintings on the rocks and their stone implements scattered about as they were lost or thrown away on the veld. Every hill and valley and little plain on this line, though now quiet and peaceful looking, has its story of battle or slaughter in the not very distant past."

He wrote that the prince, who was fond of hunting, had several opportunities of shooting antelopes on the way. The nights were somewhat cold but the days were mild and cloudless. From King William's Town, the party turned to the north, but continued through a country of ever varying and often grand scenery, where many warlike exploits could be recounted as having taken place.

The Captain described the scene of a grand hunt that had been arranged for the Prince's pleasure and diversion.

Although vast numbers of all kinds of wild animals native to this country have been destroyed for the sake of their flesh or their skins, or in mere wantonness, an immense number remain. The chief's tribesmen have been engaged for some days in driving game, and by the time we arrived it was estimated that from twenty to thirty thousand large animals --- white tailed gnus, Burchell's zebras, hartebeests, blesboks, bonteboks, springboks, ostriches, etc --- had been collected in a small area. No European prince had ever seen such a number and variety of wild animals in one spot before and no one will ever have such a sight in South Africa again, as far as I can imagine. The day of the great hunt was the most exciting one in the journey. It was not recorded how many animals were killed but it must have been a great many.

A member of the Royal party, who took an active part in the hunt, gives the following account:

The several kinds of game — ostriches, Burchell's zebras, wildebeestes, bonteboks, springboks—kept generally each kind in separate herds or droves, crossing and recrossing one another in the greatest confusion and terror, as they careered along the line seeking for a point through which they might break. A drove of wildebeestes, fierce with terror, would make a wild rush at some apparently weak point in the living fence, and— amidst clouds of dust, the falling of the dying ones, the tumbling of those living over those who were slain, the roar caused by the trampling of so many galloping feet over the ground, the bellowing of the wounded wildebeestes, the shouts and cries of the Barolongs, the continual popping of the guns and rifles —would resolutely break through the line, and madly career off into the apparently boundless plain. At some points would be seen riders falling horse and all; at others, horses whose riders were thrown, galloping here and there with the game.

The trackers formed themselves into two parties, a continuous curved line of men on either side of the long and rather deep valley which enclosed immense masses of game. The herd of animals was thus driven towards the head of the valley along the living cordon, soon rushing in confusion at full gallop, every now and again seeking in terror a point through which they might break. Then the Barolong trackers would close in at such points, riding at full gallop, shouting, shrieking and firing their guns, killing many and turning others back. As the net gradually closed in and drew nearer and nearer, the game grew more and more frantic with terror. Thus, the great moving mass of life was swept into the narrow end of the valley where the Prince's party were waiting, dismounted. Already they had been enjoying the sport of the hunt, and the Prince himself had shot 25 head of large game with his own gun. Now, they joined in the final fray with enthusiasm and the terrified animals were shot, stabbed and assegaied at close quarters while flocks of vultures hovered around and sometimes pitched onto the ground to attack a carcase.

Sandilli[2], the paramount chief of the Tambookies, with his councillors, accepted an invitation to accompany the Prince's party from Natal to Cape Town in the Emyalus. The voyage was a rough one, and the Kafirs, whose dread of the ocean is unconquerable, suffered horribly. A great impression "was made on their minds by the sight of Prince Alfred, the loved, admired, and venerated royal visitor, fresh from the triumphs and adulation of his tour through South Africa, resuming his ordinary middy's duties. They saw the boy whose coming had caused tens of thousands of hearts to beat more quickly, and had aroused unbounded enthusiasm and delight in four great States and many different races, now rising with the dawn to assist in washing down the decks. As he splashed about barefooted, all distinctions of rank merged, not in equality, but in the discipline and priority of the naval service, they wondered.

The following translation of an address, which they presented to Captain Tarloton before leaving the Euryalus, amply expresses their feelings: —

Sandilli mid his councillors give thanks. By the invitation of the great Chief, the son of the Queen of the English people, are we this day on board this mighty vessel.

The invitation was accepted with fear. With dread we came on board, and in trouble have we witnessed the dangers of the great waters, but through your skill have we passed through this tribulation.

We have seen what our ancestors heard not of. Now have we grown old and learned wisdom. The might of England has been fully illustrated to us, and now we behold our madness in taking up arms to resist the authority of our mighty and gracious Sovereign. Up to this time have we not ceased to be amazed at the wonderful things we have witnessed, and which are beyond our comprehension. But one thing we understand, the reason of England's greatness, when the son of her great Queen becomes subject to a subject that he may learn wisdom; when the sons of England's chiefs and nobles leave the homes and wealth of their fathers, and with their young Prince endure hardships and sufferings in order that they may be wise, and become a defence to their country. When we behold these things, we see why the English are a great and mighty nation.

What we have now learnt shall be transmitted to our wondering countrymen, and handed down to our children, who will be wiser than their fathers, and your mighty Queen shall be their Sovereign and ours in all time coming.

2   The Life and Times of Sir George Grey, KCB by William Lee Rees, 1892

Alexandra Bailey

Alexandra Bailey paused to study some nick-knacks in the window of the pawnbroker's shop in the High Street. She felt stiff from the overnight coach ride to Derby. After leaving the other passengers outside the inn, she walked away by herself to stretch her legs, somewhat cramped from the trip. She had not bought a present for her aunt. She felt in her pocket for some coins. She stepped inside the shop, adjusting her eyes to the darkness. There was mostly cheap stuff on display. Her perambulations took her through a doorway into a room at the back. There in the dim interior, she noticed a small portrait of an extraordinary beautiful woman. She regarded it for a minute or two. There was something familiar about the subject that she could not at first understand. She gazed at the portrait closely. Next to it on the wall was an oval mirror with a border of semi-precious stones. Alexandra looked at her reflection. Without being conscious of it, she composed her features to match those of the woman in the portrait. She looked back at the portrait, then at the mirror again. She gasped. The resemblance was uncanny.

"You must never call me Aunt. I cannot bear that appellation," were the first words that Elizabeth Atherstone uttered when she finally arrived to meet her niece off the carriage.

"Come, let's get your baggage and old Mr Waller will take us home in his buggy."

Alexandra followed Elizabeth and the porter to the vehicle waiting at the roadside.

"How is my sister?"

"Just fine. She sends her love. I have a letter for you somewhere. Oh, but it's good to get away. I feel somewhat hemmed in there."

"Of course," Elizabeth squeezed her niece's hand. "Tell me about Girl's College. Have you now completed your first year's teaching? You always said you would leave after a year. How long will you be here? And what are you going to do now? I presume they gave you a good year-end present; after all you must have been one of their star teachers. Not that I would have subscribed to their type of education."

"Yes, Aun.., yes Elizabeth." How many questions were there for her to answer?

"And no doubt, you bade farewell to your fellow teachers and promised to stay in touch with them. You won't, you know. One never does --- even your old school friend with whom you have sworn everlasting devotion. You've forgotten most of them, haven't you. You never thought of them again after a few months. Only with those who live in the district will you have retained some relationship."

Elizabeth grasped Alexandra's hand again. "It's a strange, mountainous, misty, Moorish, rocky wild part of the world. That's why I love it."

Mr Waller was resting his horse after a long uphill climb on the outskirts of the town. His two passengers, well-wrapped against the cold, studied the vista spread out before them. "That's the Peak you can see. It is noted for a cave which is named, somewhat indelicately, the Devil's Arse."

"Why, Elizabeth." Alexandra smiled. "What a coarse appellation."

Elizabeth shook her head. "Not really, given its origin. The gypsies invited the devil to a feast at the Peak, and after the meal, a vessel of Derby beer was offered to the fiend. You know that the Peak district is famous for its beer? He lifted it to his mouth and downed it in one huge draught. Then he staggered up from the table and broke wind mightily which not only blew away the remains of the banquet but caused a hole in the mountainside."

They both roared with laughter. Mr Waller coughed censoriously. He flipped the reins and the aged horse strained forward again. When they arrived at the cottage, greeted by a sheepdog and several cats, Mr Waller helped them offload Alexandra's cases. Later, tea was served in front of the fire.

"Tell me about your mother. Is she still putting up with that pompous husband of hers?"

"You don't mean that," Alexandra protested. Elizabeth had this habit of trying to shock her. Elizabeth was much younger than her sister Mary and had never disguised her displeasure over Mary's choice of marriage partner. After all, they were Atherstones, a well-known and highly respected Nottingham family. Mary still entertained members of the Moravian church at home, but only in the absence of her husband Thomas, who was a member of the James Street Independent Church.

"Well, to be married to a grain merchant is bad enough," Elizabeth continued. "But to one who is as dull as the product he sells, that's taking it too far."

"He's taken mother to the South of France for their annual holiday. That's not dull."

"Why didn't he take you as well, for goodness sake? Your father, I wager, never realized your true worth. You know, you have always contrasted greatly from your parents. Where did you get your adventurous spirit? I noticed that in you from an early age. You were a precocious reader even as a child."

Alexandra closed her eyes. She felt uncomfortable when her aunt paid what Alexandra thought were extravagant compliments --- or when she criticized her father. Yes, she acknowledged, throughout her schooling she was consistently ahead of her classmates in lessons and games. She was a natural leader too and even the boys turned to her for encouragement and advice. Now, she seemed to have lost all that.

Elizabeth went on. "You would benefit from a little broadening of the mind. Oh, I remember my first visit to Paris when I was a young girl. I decided to treat myself to a meal at Maxim's. I ordered the cheapest dish but it was still exorbitant. When I asked for the bill, the head waiter, a rather suave fellow, came to the table. He murmured in my ear: 'I am sorry, mademoiselle, it is lost'." Elizabeth shrieked with laughter at the memory. "I bet that never happened to your mother."

Alexandra flushed. She remembered that her father had remarked sarcastically, "I believe you will be spending the next fortnight with your spinster aunt." This was the sobriquet he always used when referring to Elizabeth. She had once overheard her father saying to her mother: "I am sure Elizabeth has never had a sexual experience with a man --- nor ever wanted one."

What he did not tell his wife was that when he kissed Elizabeth on the mouth one Christmas, she pushed him away with a scream and scrubbed her lips with the back of her hand. "How can you be so revolting," she had spat at him.

Alexandra was feeling disorientated. She had not slept well during the overnight coach journey. She was not fully conscious of time and place. She seemed to be in a dream. She had entered, without being aware of it, a serious crisis of self-identity. Who was that person in the painting? It could have been her sister. Or her mother. But how so?

She had to return to the shop and she took the opportunity when on a shopping trip with her aunt the following day. Elizabeth was at the greengrocers when Alexandra left her puzzling over a melon.

Isadore Solomon, for that was the name on the front window, was standing at the rear of the shop, pushing tobacco into a small pipe with a stained finger. He had an untidy beard, a hooked nose and gleaming black eyes. He laid the pipe down in a saucer, and approached them.

"I want to have a closer look at this picture. Could you move it to the light?"

Isadore Solomon took the portrait down from the wall and set it up on an easel under the front window. He moved a chair for Alexandra to sit on. He took a pair of spectacles from a case and examined the painting. He turned to Alexandra and peered at her over his glasses.

Alexandra, sitting now, gazed at the portrait. She asked quietly "And the name of the lady?"

Isadore Solomon looked at her. "I only know her name was Anna." He said. "You do look like her, don't you?"

"What do you know about this portrait?" Alexandra asked.

"The painting is by Gooch. Andrew Gooch." Mr Solomon indicated the signature at the corner of the painting. "Gooch is a well-known artist. I think he lives in this part of the world. But first you must go to see the Padre at the Moravian Church."

"Is the Moravian Church nearby," she asked her aunt later.

"Yes. Hard by the hill over there, Doak's Hill Church it is called, not far from here. The padre's wife died in childbirth. There was some scandal, I think, but I never found out the details. If you want to visit the church, I'll send Waller back in an hour to fetch you"

Alexandra paused outside the church, admiring the grey stonework. She stepped inside the dark interior and took her seat on one of the carved wooden pews. The church was empty apart from a cleaning woman who was scrubbing the steps leading from the side chapel to the vestry. Alexandra knelt in prayer then resumed her seat. She allowed her mind to drift in this haven of peace. Perhaps the painting was a fantasy. Was it just her imagination that created another person that looked just like her, that WAS her? After a while, Alexandra glanced up. The cleaning woman was watching her. She had stopped her work and was peering intently at Alexandra. Then she approached. She stood in front of Alexandra. She had clear grey eyes and there was something in her expression that puzzled the younger girl. She did not look as humble as such a menial would be expected to.

"Excuse me, young lady. May I ask you a question?"

"You may and all, except that I may not answer it."

"What is your name, pray?"

"Why do you ask? What is yours? Who are you?"

"Mrs Beecher be my name. I am the cousin of the Reverend's late wife. They were most kind to me on the death of my husband. The Reverend gave me this job as a favour. Not that my old knees are always that grateful. May I sit down?"

Alexandra gestured to her to take a seat on the pew next to her. Now her interest was aroused and she was curious as to the woman's motive. "So you have been here a long time?"

"You may count the years on your fingers and your toes. But it is really me who should be asking questions, young lady. I am sure you are not interested in an old lady's affairs. I'll tell you why I want to find out something about you because you look remarkably like someone? Would you be of the same family?"

Mrs Beecher leaned forward so that her face was at the same level as that of Alexandra's. "I ask that question because, I think, Miss Anna .... that you and her.... are of the same blood."

"Anna?"

"Yes, God rest her soul. Anna. Poor dear, you must not get upset. You look quite beside yourself. I should not have worried you. The Reverend will be cross with me. I must get back to my work."

Mrs Beecher wiped her forehead, leaving a dirty streak on her face, grasped her mop and strode out the side door of the church. Alexandra followed her.

"Please wait," she called. "I must talk to you." This was surely a message from the Lord, from someone who realised her predicament, from somewhere out of this world.

Mrs Beecher paused on the gravel path. She looked back at Alexandra, her hand shading her eyes.

"The Reverend, for all his godly ways, was .... Oh, I cannot tell you."

Then she gave a little wave of her hand, in the direction of the Vicarage, muttering to herself and shaking her head. Alexandra waited outside the church for a few moments, desperate that her means of self-identity, even if it were just a fantasy, was disappearing. Then she followed the path to the vestry at the back. She knocked on the door and waited. A man in a faded black suit and clerical collar came out. He had pale blue eyes and she realised he was half-blind.

"Reverend Hoare?" she asked. She felt quite calm as she repeated the name that was on the sign outside. He nodded and they shook hands. "My name is Alexandra Bailey and I am enquiring after something that Mrs Beecher said."

"Oh dear, has she upset you. I am sorry. She does tend to speak out of turn. Am I correct?"

Alexandra shook her head. "No. Not at all. She was most cordial. I think she mistook me for someone else. She spoke about ....."

"Anna? Is that the name?"

Alexandra nodded. Then realising the gesture would not be remarked, murmured "Yes."

"Oh, she has an obsession about Anna. No one knows who Anna is. You had better forget all about it."

Gooch, a portrait painter of much esteem, who painted the contemporary bishops and leading ministers, was a celebrated figure in the Midlands and he visited many of the mansions of the noble families in the area to execute portraits. He painted the Duke of Portland at Welbeck Abbey, the Duke of Newcastle at Clumber Park, the Duke of Norfolk at Worksop Manor and many others. Andrew Gooch steeped himself in his work with a solemn determination. He exhibited one of his most outstanding works at the Royal Academy, a portrait of Mrs Siddons. And soon after a full length portrait of the poet James Montgomery was executed for the highest commission he had ever received, one hundred and fifty guineas. This painting was also exhibited at the Royal Academy.

Alexandra had learned all this from her aunt Elizabeth. She also learnt that Andrew Gooch had never married and lived alone in a splendid house. This was in response to Alexandra's questions, asked in all innocence, whether Elizabeth knew the artist and whether she could arrange a meeting. She gave no reason for such a request and Elizabeth asked for none. She knew of her niece's interest in art and presumed this was the purpose of the visit.

Alexandra was greeted by a maid and shown into the living room. Mr

Gooch entered from another door a few minutes later. He was an extremely handsome man standing well over six feet in height, and of a very dignified aspect and graceful step. He took Alexandra's hand and kissed it.

"How are you, my dear? It has been a long time since I last saw your aunt Elizabeth..."

They faced each for a few moments. Alexandra noticed he was blushing slightly. She withdrew her hand. He frowned. "Why, you must be......"

"Anna's daughter?" Alexandra suggested. She gave Mr Gooch a searching gaze.

"Why did you not tell me? Anna..."

"My mother," Alexandra murmured. "Tell me everything you know. I must know more. And what about my father. Who was he?" she asked breathlessly.

Mr Gooch shook his head. "I honestly do not know. Elizabeth said nothing of this."

"She does not know," she said with a smile, enjoying the effect she was having on the man's composure. "Anyway, once I had seen your painting, I had to meet you."

"And your name is...?"

"Alexandra."

"Such a pretty name." Mr Gooch sounded distracted. "When did you realise you were Anna's daughter?"

"I am not sure who I am," she said, feeling helpless. "I am still trying to discover my identity."

Alexandra, until that moment, never doubted that she was the daughter of Thomas and Mary Bailey. They were older than the parents of her contemporaries. But this had never appeared to be a problem. She had enjoyed an ideal childhood. Nottingham was described many years later by Graham Greene as "a place undisturbed by ambition." But to the young Alexandra, the flower-filled valleys, the sandstone hills, the clear waters of the river Trent and the nearby legend-rich Sherwood Forest were the closest thing to heaven and all within easy reach from her parent's house on Standard Hill. The arts coloured her early environment --- literature, poetry, music, painting. Her father used to tease her. "Just because you're ugly doesn't mean you have a beautiful voice". Generally, however, he was an aloof person and it was left to her mother to recognize her daughter's talents. Alexandra, despite what her father said, did have a wonderful voice and she would sing a Thomas Moore melody with such depth of feeling that she brought tears to her mother's eyes.

"Of course, a girl must know who her mother is; especially one so pretty as you." Mr Gooch leaned over and squeezed her hand and Alexandra smiled at him.

The maid entered bearing a tray of tea and cakes. After the door closed behind her, Mr Gooch took Alexandra's elbow and led the way to the sofa. "Before we talk any further, let us enjoy a cup of tea."

"Wonderful likeness. Your mother really passed on her features. Did you suspect you were adopted?" he asked.

Alexandra nodded, shook her head and shrugged her shoulders. "I suppose I must have realised that my parents were not really my parents. But I never took it up with them."

"So your parents told you nothing about this?" He got up from his chair and paced around the room. "I am not sure if I should be telling you anything at all. But I suppose a girl needs to know who her mother is...." he repeated.

"I am going to hazard a guess that her name was Anna Hoare," Alexandra said suddenly.

"Good gracious, how did you know that?" Mr Gooch asked.

"Never mind. But was she married? No, I'm sure she could not have been. There must have been some scandal. And now I know that she is dead." She covered her face in her hands.

"Who told you?" Mr Gooch asked. "Who was it?"

"There was a strange lady at the church...."

"Oh, that must have been Aunt Beechie," Mr Gooch sighed. "What did she say?"

"Only that I reminded her of someone called Anna. Afterwards I asked the Reverend Hoare to explain. But he said Mrs Beecher was always going on about Anna and that I should forget all about it."

"She is a little touched, if that's the right word," Mr Gooch said. "Of course, your mother Anna was the padre's daughter. But he disowned her."

"Why, for pity's sake?"

"Because she had given up her faith. She was disobedient. She said she was going to leave the household in spite of his forbidding it. Actually she was pregnant and he never even knew that she was going to have a baby --- the young father was a farmer's son." Mr Gooch said. "It's not as terrible as it sounds," he added quickly, noticing Alexandra's dismay. "It was not as if she just got pregnant by some stranger."

* * *

"You will have to tell me everything now" Alexandra said firmly on her return to her aunt's home. She had taken Elizabeth by the arm and sat her down in the kitchen. "Anna Hoare. The painting by Andrew Gooch. And my parents, Thomas and Mary. I know most of it already. But I'd like you to tell me anyway."

"Good gracious. Whatever have you been up to? Are you telling me you have discovered all this while you've been here?"

"Yes, no thanks to you," Alexandra answered. She smiled to show there was no offence.

"Well then, I suppose I shall have to," Elizabeth said. "I should have paid more attention to your sleuthing around. Then I might have realised that you were on to something. Let's start with your parents, I mean Mary and Thomas. They took you into their house on my request. You know Anna died. Yes, of course you do. They adopted you. You know, of course, that neither your mother, nor I could have children?" Alexandra shook her head.

Elizabeth recounted as much as she knew, that Anna Hoare had taken a job as the doctor's assistant in Derby when she had left the vicarage; that her ambition was to go to London to study nursing as soon as she could.

Elizabeth smiled wanly. "No. Not that it mattered. It all came to nothing. Your mother, I mean Mary --- I'll have to call them Mary and Anna from now on, otherwise it's so confusing - Mary longed for a baby. And Thomas wanted someone to take over the family business in due course."

"And all they got was me," Alexandra said wryly, but she smiled.

"I remember him asking me once if I knew any Hoares around here" Elizabeth giggled. "Then he noticing what he thought was my discomfort, and he added hastily: "Any family by the name of Hoare in Derby.""

"I have already located the Reverend John Hoare," Alexandra said shortly. "And not a great deal of help was he."

"The Hoare family were great friends of the Baileys years ago," Elizabeth continued. "The padre's mother was at school with us. In fact the Baileys and the Hoares were godparents to each other's children. We seem to have drifted apart as we got older. I knew Anna Hoare vaguely as a child. She was much younger than me. Her parents were not able to send her to a good school like Girl's College. Anna went to the local day school. She took that job as a nursing assistant when she finished."

"And then she got herself pregnant?" interrupted Alexandra.

"Yes. Anna obviously realized that the situation needed to be handled with delicacy. She came to me when she knew for certain that she was going to have a baby. Of course, there was no question of adoption at that stage. Anna was determined to have the baby but was equally determined not to tell her parents at this stage. Her mother was an invalid and I believe she has since died. Her father was not the kindest and most understanding of people, and he would have been dreadfully mortified if he were to discover that his daughter was bearing a child. After all, he was the local padre."

It was while Anna was working as the doctor's assistant, Elizabeth recalled, that the turn of events that attended her would change her life.

Alexandra, lying in her bed that night, let her thoughts drift back to her aunt's account of those events. Her mother could not have been much older than Alexandra was now. She could picture her, dressed in a white uniform. Dr Skinner was about to lock up his little surgery in High Street the evening. Then a child came bursting in.

"Quick," he said, "you must come. My mother. Oh hurry."

Dr Skinner and Anna would have followed the lad out to the street where the buggy was waiting in the care of a servant. The farm was on the outskirts of the village. They would have arrived at the front door within minutes. But it was too late. The beautiful lady who had been riding side-saddle with her friend had been thrown when her horse trod in a rabbit hole. They had brought her to her room and laid her out on the bed. But her lovely white neck was quite broken and her usually pale eyelids were suffused with a dark blue which indicated a massive internal haemorrhage.

Anna would have felt a great flood of emotion when she saw the son standing at her bedside with head hung down. Quiet tears were sliding down his ravaged face. Without a thought, she would have gone to his side and put both arms on his shoulders. Their eyes locked and there passed between them a look of sympathy and tenderness. In recollection, Anna would have felt embarrassment at her boldness. She hardly knew the man and he was much older than she. She saw him next at the funeral. He came over to where she was standing and took her hands in his. They were large and warm. She looked up at him. Oh, he was so handsome. And such a tragic circumstance with his mother having died, leaving her husband and his three growing sons. She knew then that their lives would be spent together. It was only a matter of time.

Yes, that was how it would have happened. A whole year was to pass before Mr Jeremiah Hawk --- she could not call him anything else then --- came to see her one Sunday after church. The reason for Jeremiah's visit was to say goodbye.. Anna was to learn that Mr Miles Hawk had told his sons that he could never remain on his farm. He had to get right away and make a new start. He was also tempted by the promise of a whole new world --- Africa. They would leave the eldest son John to look after the affairs of the farm until it could be sold, and he and his three younger sons, Jeremiah, William and little Fred, would set sail from Southampton just as soon as they could get a berth.

Anna would have been bereft. She would have clung to his arm and begged him to confess that this was all a joke. He shook his head. But he took her home --- a rambling old stone house surrounded by an unkempt garden, a trio of sheepdogs lying in the pale sun, sweeping the ground with their gently wagging tails. The house was empty of habitation, the family were visiting relations in another part of the county --- and she felt no sin nor shame when they made love in the great bed in which his mother had died and which had not been used since that terrible occasion. Anna felt the swoop and thrust of the "wild hawk" and she cared not a whit for her own pain and the blood that stained the stiff sheets. Now we will have to get married, she said to herself as she snuggled close to her man.

All this assumed reality in Alexandra's mind. She awakened from her daydream when Aunt Elizabeth resumed her story. "When it was time for your birth, I insisted that Anna should come into my house. It was then that this painting was done. Andrew completed the work in less than a week. He gave it to her as a gift. Did she know something would go wrong? Doctor Skinner might have told her that he expected complications. Dr Skinner and the midwife arrived when Anna was due and they stayed with her the whole night. I know nothing of the details but that Anna died and you lived. The doctor asked if I knew who her parents were – and I lied. I said I did not know, but that I knew someone who could help. And that's when I called my sister.

"I knew immediately that Mary would adopt you. She told me that it took several days before she could convince Thomas. He finally agreed on the condition that Anna's father should never be told. And that you would never learn the identity of your true mother"

Elizabeth looked up. "Did I ask you if you would like a cup of tea?" Alexandra shuddered and shook her head.

"Alexandra dear, perhaps I have been wrong to tell you all this. If so, I am sorry. But I think you would have had to know sooner or later. I suppose you'll have to tell your adoptive father that I've broken my promise of silence. But you must not let it affect your relationship. You must not allow yourselves to become remote from each other."

"Why did you not tell me the painting was of my mother?" she asked Mr Solomom. "You knew who she was, didn't you. You knew I was her daughter when I came into your shop, didn't you?"

She had returned to the pawnbroker's shop to acquire the painting, however much it cost --- and however she might pay.

"How did you get it?"

Mr Solomon told her in his halting manner that Anna had come to the shop when she was very much in the family way. She looked very pale. She seemed frightened of something. She must have suspected that things might go wrong. She gave him the painting to look after. She said if she did not claim it again within a month or two, he should keep it in trust.

"She knew it would be more valuable as the years went by. She made me promise not to display it, not to sell it but to wait for someone who I would recognize as her son or daughter, and give it to that person who would reward me. If no one claimed it after 20 years, then it would be mine."

"And did she tell you the name of the man who was responsible for the child?"

He shook his head. "She never revealed his name. I could not believe anyone could be so hard-hearted as to leave Anna with a child. And then I saw you." Mr Solomom smiled shyly. He scratched his ear. "I knew right away that you must be Anna's daughter. So it is your painting now. You must just give me something of yours to remember you by."

"But I can never pay you what it is worth." Alexandra fingered the brooch on her dress. "This little bit of jewellery is all that I have. It has no real value."

"You can give it to me, nonetheless. I will treasure it from whence it came. And here's something for you." He took a little oval box of sherbert and in it he placed a gold ring hidden in a screw of pink tissue paper.

She had to pay another call on the Reverend Hoare. She resented the fact that the Reverend pretended not to know anything about Anna. Perhaps he should be taught a lesson. Alexandra, dressed carefully for the occasion, presented herself at the vicarage.

"I am your grandchild," she said quietly.

The Reverend staggered back a step. "I .... I do not know what you are saying."

"Yes," Alexandra said quietly. "My mother was Anna Hoare, your daughter whom you refuse to acknowledge." She looked. "Anna, the daughter of John

Hoare, the padre," she repeated in a whisper.

"How did you know that?" The Reverend's face was grave. "Anna was a wicked person," he said. "She abandoned me for the world of Mammon. We prayed for her. But she died. The time had come to answer for her actions."

Suddenly she realised that he was ignorant of the fact that his daughter had given birth. No wonder, even with his poor eyesight, had not recognised her as his daughter's child. It was the abandonment of her religion that condemned her in his eyes. He never knew about her love-making with Jeremiah Hawk.

"If you are worried that Anna was not married, you must not be," Alexandra said gently. "Although she did not get married to the man she loved, I am sure she would have, had she lived. I have learnt the whole story, which I have never revealed, and nor will I ever do so, to my parents nor anyone else. The man she loved was about to leave this country for ever. From the time she met him, she was completely smitten with this handsome young man and he with her. They courted for several days. Then it was time for him to leave. On their last night together, she agreed to intimacy since she was convinced that they would form a close and enduring bond. She was not worried about what you, her parents or anyone else would think. She knew that her man would return to this country, if he was not killed in battle, and then they would get married and she would follow him back to Africa to make a new life there. Of course, if he were to perish, she would have her memory of her enduring love for him."

She waited for the Reverend's response, fearing that she might have over-elaborated the story. But he remained silent, his face stony.

Alexandra said: "Never, fear. I'll not say a word about this again. But you should ask for forgiveness. You are the one who is guilty of sinning against your own flesh and blood, not Anna."

Fred and Netta Mostert

Netta Mostert watched Fred Hawk. Then she looked across the table at her grandfather as he wiped the mutton fat from his mouth with the back of his hand. She felt sick. She did not know whether it was from the rich diet or an aftermath of the terrible influenza that had taken the lives of her mother and father five years ago. Her brother was old enough to join up with another family with similar aged sons and to earn his keep by hunting. There were eight families in all who trekked north that year from the settlements in the Cradock area of the Cape. Netta remained behind with her grandparents. Her grandfather had acquired several fat-tailed sheep from the Hottentots. These flocks now grazed in the flat plains under the eye of the little Hottentot herd-boys. The Boers were voracious meat-eaters, the larger households slaughtering and consuming three or four sheep a day. Mutton comprised almost their entire diet due to their nomadic habits and their reluctance or inability to establish crops.

They were the coarsest and least-educated of the European colonists. For half of the year they drove their sheep into the remote grasslands in search of grazing, each family needing only a wagon, a span of oxen and a few goats to supply milk. They were as rugged and as independent as Arabs in the Saharan desert. They made their own clothes--- leather jackets and trousers, velschoene (literally, skin shoes) --- and their dwellings were unfurnished and wretchedly small. The Mosterts, who were regarded as the leaders of the community, had taken the trouble to erect a more substantial home.

It was a Sunday and Netta was out walking with the family sheepdog. Fred came riding out from the plain with his Hottentot servant at his side. The dog immediately attacked Fred's horse which reared back in fright. But he quickly brought the animal under control and dismounted. "Ek is jammer, Meneer." Netta said to him. At the same time she threw a stick at the dog which came to heel.

"Well, and who might you be?" asked Fred in Dutch. He had been occupied for the best part of the day surveying the northern boundaries of the farm. He was not aware of any squatters living in this area. "Netta Mostert," she answered with a little curtsy. She sensed from his demeanour that he was the owner of the land. Her grandfather had often remarked about the Englishman who had taken possession of "their" land. For years the Boer farmers had regarded it as common pasture where they could run their flocks.

Netta admired Fred's huge black horse. She squinted at him in the sunshine." Do you live nearby?" he asked her.

"Ja," she answered.

"Show me your home."

Netta led him reluctantly in the direction of their rough homestead. What would her grandfather say? The Englishman would have to evict them, she concluded. She glanced at him again as he walked slowly behind her, leading his horse. The Hottentot followed discreetly a few paces behind. They drew up at the door and Netta called softly "Oupa, oupa." Her grandfather came out. He welcomed Fred courteously. He held out his hand. "Mostert," he said, by way of introduction. "Hawk," Fred responded. His wife and granddaughter stood deferentially aside when Fred was escorted into the room. The Mostert home was rather a narrow building, about twelve feet wide and forty long, with a thatched roof and mud ridging, the supporting timbers being rough un-sawn poles cut in the bush. It was divided into three rooms: the sitkamer (living room) into which one entered being the largest, then the kombuis (kitchen) leading off to the left with its own separate entrance at the back for the servant, and the bedroom (slaapkamer) on the right. In the voorkamer, the furniture consisted of a rough wooden table, several chairs whose seats were made from riempie (thin strips of cured hide) and a home-made rusbank or couch, also with riempie seat and back. There were also large voorkisten, wooden boxes, which held all their clothing and other possessions. In the corner of the room were yokes and gear for sixteen oxen, beautifully made yoke skeys (jukskei was already well-developed as a community game), reims and strops. A wagon whip on a long pole was placed on top of the rafter beam as was the farmer's saddle and bridle. The trek tow was made not of chain but twisted hide, strong and light. The Voortrekker wagon itself stood outside. The wooden-framed kartel which forms the bed when travelling had of course been lifted out and placed in the house. There it was supported by four forked posts planted in the floor of the bedroom. The canvas sail of the wagon had also been taken off and carefully stored in the house. The bedclothes consisted of karosses, or animal skins. Within easy reach of the bed was the muzzle-loader and hanging from a peg on the wall was a powder horn fashioned from the thick straight horn of an eland. Next to it was a leather haversack containing the leather wads which had been soaked in melted fat, percussion caps, round leaden bullets and shot. There was also a supply of vet-lappies (greased linen patches used to wrap the round bullets when loading). The kitchen had an open wood-burning stove and the major cooking utensil was a flat bottomed pot for baking bread. The floor of the entire house was mud smeared with cow dung with a number of animal skin mats-including one of a lion.

Fred accepted Mostert's invitation to join the family in the partaking of their midday meal. This was preceded by the saying of grace. Regardless of their physical living conditions, they were God-fearing people. One of old Mostert's most valuable possessions was a massive old Bible. He pronounced the prayers while Netta read from the scriptures. She had received a rudimentary education at a mission school in the Cape. The dedication was also attended by two black servants who withdrew when it was over.

"Meneer Mostert." Fred cleared his throat. They had finished the meal and were drinking coffee on the stoep. "I think you know that our family owns this land now."

"Ja. I understand. I have been coming here with my sheep for five years now. I hope you understand too." The old man was not hostile.

"Perhaps we can come to some agreement. I will have to talk to my brother." They shook hands and Fred called for his servant to bring the horses. As he mounted, Netta came out the front door. She looked sad and helpless and Fred, without thinking said: "Would you like to come for a ride with me?"

"I cannot. Today is Sunday."

"Tomorrow, then."

"I do not have a proper horse."

"I'll bring a horse. You can ride, can't you?"

"Of course."

"Tomorrow. I will be here at ten o'clock." She did not answer, and slipped back into the house.

When Fred rode out to the Mostert home that morning, he had some difficulty in controlling the second horse. He had to keep jerking the reins to keep it from pulling away from him. But when Netta mounted the pony, she sat astride with ease.

"Come, let's take a rest here," Fred suggested. They had been in the saddle for nearly an hour. He held Netta's horse while she dismounted then took her hand. Netta was intensely shy. They tethered the horses and sat down in the grass looking up into the foliage of the trees. Nervously, she spoke. "Why not ask the old man to help you on the farm. If you make him leave here, he will die."

Fred looked at her in surprise. He pondered what she had said. Could old Mostert develop the sheep farming activities on the ranch? Fred had earmarked an area of twenty thousand acres extending from the homestead at Iron Crown right into the desert. Here the carrying capacity was only one animal to 10 acres. Could old Mostert take charge of this area?

"Well, the old man is living on our property and is running sheep on our land. It must not continue. But we would hate to deprive anyone of his living." Fred was conscious that might sound insincere. He looked away to hide his embarrassment. "I do not know whether he would like to farm for somebody else. Especially an Englishman," he added under his breath. "Our way of farming will be very different," he continued. "Maybe he would not want to." He looked at Netta. She just looked back at him. "Well, maybe he would," Fred reflected. Just as long as he combined modern techniques with the traditional pastoral know how of the Boers.

"We will certainly think about it. Please ask your grandfather to call on my brother. Tell him he might have a proposal for him." Fred felt he was already going too far. He hadn't even discussed the idea with his brother who might dismiss it out of hand. Fred knew his attitude towards Boer farmers. Netta suddenly leaned over and kissed him lightly on the cheek. Fred blushed.

"Will you please not say it was me who suggested it," Netta asked quietly. Fred promised. "Can I see you again? You know, we can talk about ...things." "Ja. I would like that. The old people always eat at sundown. Then they go to bed."

They remained at the spot under the trees for a long while, not saying anything. Fred held her hand. She tickled his nose with a blade of grass. Then she said: "Kom, ons moet gaan." They rode back together and Fred departed with both horses.

Next day they went riding again. Fred told Netta about England, how different it was to the stark countryside of the Cape. He recited some verses of Keats ---"season of mists and mellow fruitfulness." To her, with her limited knowledge of English, his words sounded like water rippling over the stones in a stream. She tried to imitate his speech and he gently corrected her pronunciation and misuse of words. She had never known anyone so courteous and attentive. He even took her hand when they traversed the steps in the garden. Netta marvelled at the softness of his skin. "It's the oil from the wool," he told her. "Have you never felt it? Come, I'll show you."

He took her to the shearing shed where there were a number of bales open on the floor. "Feel it," he said, offering her an armful of the fragrant wool. She rubbed it on her hands and held it against her face. On an impulse, Fred lifted her with strong arms onto a half-filled woolsack. The delicious feel of the wool sent her into transports of delight. He laughed at her pleasure. "It's wonderful. D'you think that's how the sheep feel?"

She coaxed him into the wool bale with her. They rubbed handfuls of wool on each other's faces. Then she opened his shirt front and rubbed his chest. He pushed a handful down her blouse. Suddenly they were scared. There was a strange wildness developing. Must they stop? Fred lay back, his eyes closed. The bale of wool lay on its side, its contents spilled out on the floor. Netta felt her bosoms heaving with an unaccustomed pressure. She felt she had to loosen her blouse. Without realising it, she released two lovely wobbling pink breasts. She covered them with wool scooped up. Fred leaned over and cupped each breast with a hand. Then he kissed them, one by one. Netta felt the blood rising to her face.

"I'm so hot," she said. She wriggled out of her dress. Fred pressed wool all about her. Her legs seemed to want to spread wide. She helped him unbutton his shirt. And his trousers. Fred knelt in the wool, positioning himself over her. He groaned and twisted his head one way and then the other.

"It's all right," she said. "Come into me." She guided him in with unsure hands. She felt the sudden hot spurting of his loins before he had properly entered her body, and at the same time, tears sprung from his eyes.

"Don't worry," she soothed. "Everything's all right. Cry if you like. It must be very difficult for you."

Fred fell back. Netta eased herself from beneath him. She squatted in the wool next to him. She took a handful of soft wool and mopped the sticky substance from his belly and hers. She watched as his body straightened and seemed to grow. He groaned again. With a cry in her own throat, she covered him with her body, feeling the urgency of him. This time he was able to enter. He lay still while she moved above him. His arms thrust outwards and his hands grabbed into the wool. Now she felt her own desire. Now she thrust at him herself. She strained upwards in a backward-arching movement, at the same time gently rocking backward and forward. Then he leaned forward and upward, grabbed her around the waist and started thrusting himself. She couldn't seem to widen her legs enough. He was piercing her with pain and ecstasy. She started a strange cooing noise in her throat. Then her eyes rolled back and she blacked out in an unbelievable indescribable welling of unknown feeling.

The Ostrich

The ostrich. The world's largest living bird, a member of the order of Struthioni forms which includes kiwi, emu, rhea and casserwari. The adult male, weighing up to 300 pounds, lives for 60 years in favourable circumstances. Standing up to eight feet in height (mostly being made up of a long dun-coloured neck) he will either fight like a lion or flee like an abject coward. In his aggressive mood, he will attack directly head-on with a rally of blows from his long and powerful legs, his two-toed feet capable of inflicting vicious wounds. And when he is on the defensive, he will run with unbelievable swiftness, shaking from side to side, with his shaggy feathers in great bundles about his shoulders, at speeds of 40 miles per hour or more.

Two-toed? The African ostrich is quite unique in the number of his toes. All the other bird species have four toes, and even his Australian and American cousins have three. This is taken to be a sign of degeneration in the genus of Ratitea or running bird.

And the feathers? In reality, the ostrich is a very scantily covered bird, and the few feathers that he has are fluffy. They offer no resistance to the air in open flue so he is quite unable to lift himself off the ground, even momentarily. The under surface of the wing and the leg are quite featherless, and the head is almost bald. In fact, in hot weather when he spreads his wings on the ground, he looks quite naked.

The ostrich has not enjoyed a good press. HV Morton[3] relates a meeting with a farmer in Oudtshoorn:

3   Morton HV, In Search of South Africa, Metheun, London, 1948

He told me that the ostrich is the most stupid of all birds; in fact he almost doubted if it had a brain. So far as I could gather, it is merely a fuselage covered with feathers, mounted on a pair of tremendous limbs and with an expression of perpetual apprehension beneath its enormous Hollywood lashes. Apart from stupidity and vanity, the only other human attribute which the ostrich possesses is a love of dancing. Sometimes when the birds are let out from the kraal in the morning, they sail off, feeling good, revolving together in a waltz; some, however, become giddy, fall down and break their legs and have to be shot.

Fred was yet to learn all of this. But he did, and a lot more during the next decade in which ostrich farming became very popular in the Cape. And it was by coincidence that it all started. Fred was on one of his nature rambles on a Saturday afternoon, on horseback and well beyond the borders of the farm.

He came across a Boer farmer, an itinerant grazier who drove his sheep and goats northwards in the summer to seek pastures which were not already occupied by his neighbours. The old man sat on the driving seat of a covered wagon. He had a few dogs with him, a muzzle loader and, of all things, a tame ostrich hen. She was tethered with a long riempie to the wagon but was quite unperturbed except when one of the dogs yapped too close to her, at which time she would swing her head menacingly at the animal.

The old man could hardly speak English, and they greeted each other in patois Dutch. The old man came this way every year and spent several months ranging over the open veld, content in his isolation And the ostrich? Yes, a fine bird. Every year one of the wild ostrich cocks would come down from the hills and mate with her, thus assuring the old man a clutch of eggs, most of which would be hatched into chicks. And the riempie? Why, that was to prevent the precious bird from eloping with her lover.

"Die laaste een het met the wildhaan weggehardloop," he chuckled.

Fred asked him about the eggs. Did he have any?

"Het u eiers nodig?"

"Ja." Fred certainly did want to obtain some ostrich eggs. "Mijneer. Weet Mijneer waar 'n mens so a klomp kan kry?"

"Ek weet. As u daarvoor betaal."

Fred had no resources to pay for such information but something would come up, he was convinced.

"Kom." The old man indicated that Fred should dismount. He in turn called the Hottentot lad to mind the oxen and climbed down stiffly from the driving seat. He pulled aside the canvas cover at the back of the wagon. He showed Fred a hessian bag containing ostrich eggs.

"Hierdie is oud" he told Fred. But he knew where fresh eggs could be obtained. Twenty fertile ostrich eggs would cost Fred a gold sovereign.

The old man said he would have two Cape men the following day. "Hulle is Hotnots wat weet waar hulle die eiers van 'n wilde volstruis kan kry." Fred was to return, with his horse and buggy and the men would show him where he could obtain the eggs of a wild ostrich. He had to be prepared to travel for some distance into the desert, and it would help if he brought a few items to barter with the Bushmen. Fred was to leave half the agreed amount with the man and the other half would be payable on his return, with the eggs.

It took Fred and the old Boer farmer's two servants three days steady travel to reach the designated spot. It was a waterhole in the desert, and they camped there for another two days before a family of Khoi appeared. One of the Cape men spoke to them in their language for some while. Then he came back to Fred. "They want to see what you give them for 20 eggs." Fred opened the case that Aaron had prepared for him. In it were packets of tobacco, a well-made knife in a sheath, a string of blue beads, a mirror, a small tin box and a brightly coloured shawl. The Khoi crowded around to look. The items were passed from one hand to another. Finally their leader indicated that the knife was the choice. The Cape man told Fred that he should put away the rest.

"No, all of this is for them." The Cape man violently disagreed. "Next time they will expect the same," he said. But Fred was adamant. He felt embarrassed enough exchanging these few items for something that would be of great value to him. Eventually he agreed to divide the tobacco amongst the Cape men as well as the Khoi. The latter of course were overjoyed with their good fortune, and the women did an impromptu dance for the visitor.

The Khoi needed a week to collect 20 ostrich eggs. They left their bartered goods with the Cape men and set off on their quest. Ostrich eggs were an extremely important commodity for the Khoi. Not only were they a source of nourishment, but more importantly, they were the receptacles for carrying and storing their precious supplies of water. So the little men had developed egg collection into a fine art. They would not pass on their secrets to anyone else, not that others were really in a position to copy them. It was said by those who purported to know, that the nest thief would stalk right up to the sitting bird holding a stick aloft and clutching a bunch of ostrich feathers in front of him. Then he would actually remove the eggs from under the hen by stealth.

There would usually be 10 or 12 eggs in a full clutch but the Khoi would only take three or four. Next day more would be laid and the little man would again remove some. The ostrich would lay up to 30 eggs at one sitting while they were constantly being depleted in this way.

In due time, the Khoi returned with the eggs and Fred and his companions set off on the return trip with the eggs covered in sacks at the back of the buggy. These sacks were continually exchanged for others draped over the back of the horses (which were extremely uncomfortable under their unaccustomed blankets). Their first port of call was the old Boer farmer. He accepted the balance of his price, with a courteous nod. Then he called out to a group of Hottentots who were sitting nearby. A large woman got up, adjusting her blanket round her frame. He told Fred that she would be the foster mother; that she would stay in a backroom at the homestead for the entire period of incubation, lying in a bed with the eggs. Forty days and forty nights, that would be, less the few days since they were laid by the ostrich hen.

One of the woman's companions would come every morning with food, and she would take her turn while the other went off to relieve herself. Fred wondered at the patience of the surrogate hen and her calm acceptance of her role. It must have been mightily tedious and uncomfortable in the hot weather.

Meanwhile, the first eggs began hatching. Sixteen of the 20 eggs yielded chicks which were indistinguishable from each other when they broke through the sturdy eggshells. Fred kept them in an enclosure and walked among them every day to get them accustomed to human presence. The warm climate of Iron Crown, the crisp dry air and sandy soil all made for ideal conditions for the rearing of the birds. They received a varied diet --- chopped aloes, mealies and lucerne, prickly pear leaves, even crushed bone. This was the menu suggested by the Boer who occasionally called at the farm to see how "his" birds were getting on. He showed Fred how to crush bones to a consistency suitable for ingestion by the chicks. He told Fred they needed this to grind their food. If he did not give it to them, they would try to swallow stones and other rough objects which might injure them.

The ostrich legend goes right back to the earliest days of recorded Egyptian history. There was frequent mention in hieroglyphics of the ostrich feather as the symbol of justice. Did you know that this is the only feather of all birds anywhere which is perfectly even on both sides? A specimen was found at Thebes in the sepulchral chamber of the 18th dynasty, which puts it contemporary with Moses. Arsubie, the queen before Cleopatra, had a statue of herself riding an ostrich. It was called a camel bird, a term that is still used by the Arabs.

The Syrians still believe that the ostrich is a holy bird. Before the Crusades, the plumes were only to be worn by kings and military leaders, along with the feathers of peacocks and eagles. Then the invading knights adopted the practice of wearing plumes in their helmets. This became very fashionable in the Middle Ages, but it was still a practice confined to the nobility and the high-born. It was only after the 17th Century that it became popular with the female of the species. In Queen Elizabeth's reign, the ladies at court started wearing feathers in their gowns. The Prince of Wales adopted a badge of three white ostrich feathers which to this day has remained unchanged. Marie Antoinette wore ostrich plumes too.

Egypt pioneered the practice of ostrich farming. There the ostriches were hunted by the aristocracy on horseback. This was particularly simple when they were nesting since the females would refuse to leave the nest. The hunter would ride right up to the hen and shoot her as she sat on the eggs. But they would not remove her because, soon afterwards, the male would show up. And he would also be killed.

Even the peasant would hunt ostriches in the desert. He would hide behind a screen made of ostrich skin, and gradually approach a group of birds. When he was near enough he would drop his disguise and hurl a stick with great force and skill at the nearest ostrich and thus break its legs.

Fred spent an inordinately large proportion of his time with his young charges. It was a tedious period until the birds were old enough to crop. He constructed a double fence five foot high to ensure that the birds, when adult, would not escape. They were rovers by nature and would seek to return to their wild state if they could. Fred learnt how to cope with the occasional disease such as dronksiekte or giddiness. When there was an influx of tapeworm, he starved the ostrich chicks for two days then gave them turpentine.

But at last the feathers began to assume colour, and one could distinguish between the cocks with their bold black and white plumes and the hens with their modest grey hues. He carefully examined the feathers with the upper plume bearing the flue, the soft fluffy part, and the lower being the quill. The first row of wing plumes from the young bird was the most valuable, being white, while the second and third rows were black. Only those three rows of the wing feathers and those of the tail were to be clipped.

One by one the birds were driven into a wooden enclosure and a sock like cloth was pulled over their heads. Prima is the first grade finest quality cut quill ---Prima best, Prima long, Prima ordinary --- these were the classifications by which the feathers would be sold at the quarterly auctions. Plumes from the hen were known as Femme and were graded light, usual, half dark and dark. Then there are byocks, which are white with black spots, and blacks. Spadonas are the lowest classification, being the most drab.

At the end of the first year, each of the birds had produced 200 commercial feathers. Henceforth they would be plucked every eight months and the yield would increase by 50 per cent or more. And with the prices at the equivalent of 100 dollars a pound, this was an undreamed of source of wealth for Iron Crown.

"We need two things," Fred said to himself. "We need some first class breeding stock from outside this country. And we need an incubator. We can get 200 eggs from our flock right now and if we get 80 per cent incubation, then we can start selling breeding birds as well as boosting our own stock."

He knew that the Barbary ostriches were highly valued. They were captured in great quantities and sold from Tripoli by private contract. Buyers in the Cape could obtain supplies via Marseilles for cross breeding with the local strain. This would, he was sure, be a powerful incentive for the local ostrich industry. There was also a good source at Aleppo in the Syrian Desert but the Syrians believed that the ostrich was holy. The cocks of the northern end of the continent had feathers of a very much purer white than their cousins of the south.

This is one reason why ostrich farming is so fascinating. It is steeped in myth, romance and perhaps even decadence. Diamonds were yet to be found in the blue kimberlite clay not far from Iron Crown. And diamonds and ostrich feathers were soon to be the most important industries in the country. Does this indicate a distortion of values? Is man's love of display, or rather woman's, quite necessary in respect of the good of mankind? Ornamental and decorative. It's quite ridiculous really.

The ostrich business was booming. Fred was now running a flock of several thousand. Top quality primas were now fetching 30 pounds per lb, a five-fold increase in just 18 months. He had just purchased a breeding cock, the best in the land, for over £1 000. He was astounded at the extent of his income.

The Cape became far and away the greatest producer of ostrich feathers for the fashion industry. It was the most lucrative branch of farming and only slightly exceeded in export values by wool. Fred, who had become blinded by the size and apparent success of his operations, did not foresee the clouds beginning to gather on the horizon. First, quality control began to wane. Anyone could start an ostrich farm. The capital costs were not high. There was a fast stock increase. There was less work involved than in other branches of farming and even a lazy man could make a good living. And so, overproduction became another factor in the slide. No effort was made within the country to promote the industry which depended on fashions made popular in other countries. In fact, the society ladies in the Cape were not a whit interested in ostrich feathers --- "even the natives wear them."

There was an influx of inferior stock, a fall in demand, and a change in fashion. The anti-plumage campaign in England also had an effect on the situation. The good ladies of Bloomsbury, (who was to say whether their inability to afford the splendid feathers contributed to their attitudes) protested against the slaughter of beautiful birds (although the birds were clearly not killed for their plumes). They demonstrated against the cruelty of ostrich plucking (although the feathers were carefully clipped).

The advent of the motor car was probably more instrumental in changing fashions. There was no way that a woman could wear with her usual dignity the elaborate hats in a vehicle, even at 10 miles per hour.

The fault, however, lay squarely with the producers in the Cape. No funds were collected to promote ostrich feathers for other uses, such as trimming dresses and coats, or even handbags. No counter was given to competitive articles such as flowers and ribbons. The French fashion industry, which affected the whole of Europe, could well have received massive assistance from the flowing coffers of the ostrich farmers.

Finally and inevitably, the ostrich farmers lost everything. Overnight, entire herds were released because the farmer could not afford to pay his labour. Breeding cocks purchased for huge sums of money were suddenly worthless. The industry went bankrupt, dragging down many farmers, agents, exporters and the countless middlemen who had made a handsome living out of the ill-fated venture. Iron Crown was amongst the hardest hit.

The Siege of Bathhurst

On the night before the full-scale invasion of warriors, the Bowlers got the tip-off from the old Cape herdsman who lived on the edge of the plain which served as a pasture for the sheep. He was a frail old fellow who was in Miles Bowler's debt, so to speak, having been saved from certain drowning during their journey from the south when one of the streams came down in flood. Bowler had ridden his horse into the torrent and somehow managed to scoop the old man onto the saddle.

That night old Kleinbooi came and tapped on the kitchen door. The family had already gone to bed but eventually Anna Maria came and let him in.

"The impi he is coming," he told her. "The baas take you and the children away. Quick."

The family was quickly assembled in the dining room and a plan of action made. Guy Hawk decided that the house was too vulnerable to be properly defended. They should move out in case there was an attack at first light. The Hottentot servants were summoned --- they were equally terrified of the invaders and would surely be put to the spear. Hermanus, the head servant of the household, took charge of the preparations for departure. He sent two of his men down to the cattle kraal to round up the trek oxen, no easy task in the pitch dark, and inspan the big 30-foot wagon. Hermanus's wife, Katrina, returned to the servants' quarters to arouse the women and children. They could take only those belongings which could easily be carried. The little children would be found a place on the wagon. Orders were given to the herdsmen to evacuate the cattle and sheep from the thorn bush enclosures where they were quartered every night and move them out into the open fields. At first light the stock should be driven as quickly as possible away from the river. But they must stay together and not split up into small parties.

Meanwhile Anna Maria directed her three sons, John, Jeremiah and little Fred to collect all the family silver and other valuables. Baby Jocelyn was excited by the adventure and brought her own collection of treasures to the dining room table --- bound up in a silk scarf. The boys made several trips to and from the bedroom and the front lounge --- the voorkamer --- with heirlooms from England, jewellery, ivory, some old paintings, an antique canteen of silver, the willow-pattern china, gold coins and medals, even the family bible. Everything was wrapped up in a huge damask tablecloth and loaded carefully onto a handcart. The two elder Hawk boys could only just manage the heavy load and struggled off into the darkness, little Fred bringing up the rear with a large shovel. After several hundred yards, they took a path off into some thick bush and by chance came across a huge ant-bear hole. The booty was lowered in, still wrapped in the huge tablecloth, and Stephen took the shovel to complete the burial. As he started to heap soil into the hole, the rain started to fall.

"You must be quick," little Fred urged. "The kaffirs are coming."

A terrific flash of lightning lit up the sky and the boys, with one accord, fled. They did not retrace their steps along the path but ran directly towards the homestead, Jeremiah pushing the hand cart in front of him, making their way through the bushes lit up by the successive sheets of lightning. The menfolk had by now saddled up their horses. Led by Mr Hawk, they escorted the wagon away from the homestead, down the usually dusty road which had now been turned by the rain into a slippery river of mud.

"Where are we going?" Anna Maria asked. "Back to Bathurst. We must stand together," her husband responded. He wheeled his horse and cantered ahead. The wagon containing the Hawk family and their servants, its progress slowed by the darkness and rain, reached the village just after daybreak. They were greeted by several dozen farmers' wives, some of whom were in a great state of agitation as they had also been warned of the invading impis.

"Let us hope and pray that it is more of a cattle raid than an attack," said George Sewell who owned the trading store. "You should just move here for a few days and let them take your stock."

But Guy Hawk shook his head. "No, we cannot just let our possessions be stolen like that. Now that Anna Maria and the little ones are safe with you, the lads and I will go back and investigate. The Hottentots cannot be relied upon entirely to defend our possessions." Several of the farmers elected to accompany the Bowlers. The menfolk were used to the calling up at short notice of a commando to reconnoitre the outlying farms.

"Right, let's get moving, "Hawk called out and the group cantered off down the muddy road.

They soon came upon large herd of cattle being driven slowly towards them by Hottentot herdsmen. These were the remains of the settlers stock, many of which had been easy prey to the marauders who would cause a diversion, isolate a section of the herd and then drive the confused animals away. They would repeat this exercise again and again, always keeping out of the way of the herdsmen, some of whom were armed. When Miles Bowler and party came upon the scene, the raiders slipped away. Mr Bowler beckoned to three of the farmers who were armed. "Come on, lads. Let's speed them on their way. William, you and Stephen take that way and I'll go this way with our good men. Do not get too close and do not dismount. Fire when you are sure you can hit your target. If we get separated, remember, we must be back at Bathurst by nightfall." Guy Hawk chose to accompany the boys.

After cantering through the valley, they arrived at a rocky ravine, and reined in their horses. Guy Hawk, shielding his eyes with his hand, pointed upwards. A large group of natives could be seen climbing towards a cave, high up on one side of the gorge, Mr Hawk quickly sized up the situation. "We'll go up on top of that krantz, directly opposite the cave mouth. We'll shoot them out."

His plan was simple, and effective. He led the boys up the krantz directly facing the cave mouth and, at the signal, they fired several bursts of gunfire into the opening. There was immediate consternation within. The bullets either found their mark directly or ricocheted from rock to rock, causing death or serious wounds to all the fugitives. Six, seven, eight bodies rolled down through the mouth of the cave and slithered down the rock face, rolling and sliding, crashing through the bushes to end up at the foot of the cliff. A second and a third volley was fired until there were no sounds within.

Jeremiah and John scaled nimbly down the rock face to observe at close quarters the dreadful carnage caused by the gunfire --- half-naked men, covered in blood, dust, faeces and vomit. Guy Hawk joined them. "You wait here," he told the boys. "Keep your guns at the ready but for God's sake do not fire unless I tell you." He placed his own gun on a rock and cautiously examined the corpses. He picked up a crude knife from the dust. Suddenly there was a movement from one of the apparently lifeless bodies, lying against a rock. Guy Hawk laid hold of an ankle, but the man rolled away and attempted to stand up. Guy called out and at the same time lunged at the man with the knife he was still clutching. But the knife blade was soft and it rolled up like a piece of hoop iron. The native turned on him with an upraised assegai and it was Guy's turn to double up and roll away. Jeremiah, who was watching nervously, realising he could not use his gun in such a confined space, grasped a large stone and aiming at the black man's head, he flung it with all his might. But the man ducked and the stone splintered against the rock face. He leapt towards the man to grapple with him. "Down, down." The voice of his father came over him like a thunder clap. He ducked down to the ground and rolled away. A volley of fire cracked out, echoing and reverberating against the cliff. The luckless native fell soundlessly in the dust.

The party regrouped and set out on the return journey, Hawk riding ahead. John and Jeremiah were feeling a little light-headed after their adventure. Hawk urged his mount into a gallop when he saw some cattle near a clump of bushes. These must have escaped the attention of the marauders, he said to himself. He reined in to inspect the scene. Just then, four desperate blacks broke cover from the bushes and ran frantically across the field in front of him. Hawk immediately dismounted and knelt, aimed carefully and fired. One of the fleeing natives dropped to the ground. Suddenly, the three remaining men turned on their pursuer. They must have realised what had happened. In a classic manoeuvre which must have accounted for many an enemy in a tribal battle, two of the warriors wheeled away on either side of Hawk then turned and grabbed his arms, spread-eagling him. The third took his short assegai in both hands and lunged at the man with a killer stab aimed at the pit of the neck.

With superhuman effort, Hawk jerked back and the assegai ripped into his leather jacket and became entangled in his belt. He fell to the ground like a stone.

In the few seconds that it took for all this to happen, Jeremiah spurred his horse forward to the scene of the struggle. He quickly loaded a charge of buckshot into his double-barrelled smooth-bore musket, and fired it at the three natives who were standing over the fallen figure. He aimed as high as he could to avoid hitting his father --- was he still alive? --- with the result that his entire charge ripped into the enemy at head height, instantly killing all three.

Hawk was moaning and clutching his stomach. Blood had already soaked through his clothes and his hands were bright red when he withdrew them. It was a deep wound, the tip of the spear having lodged itself in his broad leather belt, and entered his belly.

He was able to remount his horse which Jeremiah had gone back to fetch. They rode back to the village together but by the time they arrived, Hawk was white-faced from loss of blood and swaying dangerously in the saddle. The boys called Anna Maria for aid and she disinfected and dressed the wound. But he could hardly stand and she summoned George Sewell to inspect the wound.

"We'll have to get him to hospital in Grahamstown. With any luck we will have driven off these savages by tomorrow."

But the marauding Xhosas who had been encountered were forerunners of the main party and a great horde of warriors were drawing themselves into their traditional formation. "They will surely attack us as soon as night falls," Mr Sewell said flatly. "For defensive purposes, we will have to fortify positions in front of the church. The women and children must take refuge inside. Will that be all right, Reverend Shaw?" The priest nodded. "I will stay with them."

"Thank you. Now for the rest of you. Come let us see to the guns. We will need several of the more reliable servants to load for us. The rest of us will do the shooting."

The guns were the trusty flint-locks, and they were carefully laid out together with the necessary powder horns and bags of lead bullets. Additional supplies of lead as well as the moulds for making bullets were also set out. The smooth-bored flint-lock muzzle loaders were generally known as a tower musket from the little 'tower' stamped on the side. George Sewell showed the loading party how to prepare the guns. "First you measure out a charge of black powder from this powder horn onto the palm of your hand, like this. Then you pour it down the barrel, so, and follow it with one of these round lead balls. On top of this goes this wad of a grease rag --- and this you rammed tight with a ram. Then while we are waiting to fire, you must mould new lead balls on the fire here. This is the mould. You fill it with molten lead from this pot. And you cool it with water, like this. Do you think you can manage?"

"They had better," Sewell said to himself quietly. "Otherwise we are lost."

Although his own accuracy with these primitive weapons was almost uncanny, he could not vouch for the others, especially the younger men who had not been subject to such extreme circumstances. And the loaders were crucial to the whole enterprise.

"Yes, but we will have to find a way of speeding up the moulding process. It takes too long. What about this." Quickly he whittled a peg of wood the right size and pressed it into the ash around the fire, making a number of holes. These he filled with the molten lead and lo, they had 20 bullets. The Rev Shaw looked at him with respect. He carefully picked up one of the bullets with a cloth and examined it.

"By God, George. You have made the most remarkable discovery."

None of them were to know it then but George Sewell had not only managed to increase the production rate of bullets twentyfold but the bullets themselves, being conical in shape, proved to be more accurate and they also travelled farther than the round bullets. This development was subsequently reported to the military authorities in Grahamstown and the army adopted the new method.

When the warriors started their war dances, beating their bare feet on the dusty ground, and ululating, the effect on the women in the church was initially one of great shock and fear. The Reverend Shaw rallied them around him. Apart from the priest, Anna Maria, baby Jocelyn, and the grievously wounded Guy Hawk,, there were 20 women and children who were milling about and whimpering. "It's no good going on like this. We have to stand fast. That's all there is to it. The men are out there and they'll take the brunt of the attack." The priest came forward and said: "What is more, we're in the Lord's house and He will take care of us."

The men had meanwhile settled down in their positions behind the low wall of the churchyard. They had not long to wait before the first attack was mounted. "Do not fire until I say so," shouted Bowler. Then, as the first wave of black warriors stormed their laager, he screamed "Fire."

The attackers were beaten back by the sustained gunfire, but after the first volley, there was a heart-stopping delay while molten lead was poured into the round moulds. If the bullets weren't ready for the next attack, the settlers would surely be overrun. Luckily the natives did not realise this, and they took several minutes to gather their forces before the next charge.

Although the Rev Shaw succeeded in calming the womenfolk inside the church, it was Anna Maria who saved them from certain death. She noticed the hundreds of flickering lights in the darkness. They're going to try to burn us out, she thought. She looked up at the thick thatch that comprised the church roof. Dry as tinder, it would burn fiercely and the heat and smoke would surely suffocate everyone within. The doors had already been barricaded from without and the only ready exit was a small window. She whispered to the Rev. Shaw who nodded.

"We will have to tear down the thatch roof," he announced. "We cannot afford the risk of having it fired over our heads. Those natives will throw brands onto the roof if they can get near enough."

So they got to work. Several heavy wooden pews were used to make a platform and the taller women were then able to reach the inside of the roof. It was difficult to start with, since they had to claw and scratch a hole in the thick grass. But after that it was easier and the bundles of thatch came away readily. Young Fred was thrust through the window and armloads of thatch were handed to him.

"Take them down to the spring next to the wall," Anna Maria told him. "Put them in the water."

The youth staggered along, with several bundles in his arms, and deposited them in the water. Soon the pile grew and completely obliterated the spring. Then Frederick took a bucket and flung water over the grass. His arms were scratched and raw from his labours but he carried on without complaint. Finally the job was done. The women shivered in the cold of the roofless building. The pews were all pushed to the near wall and the floor swept of all the grass.

"We must all stand against this near wall, on top of the pews. When a burning torch comes through the roof, whoever is nearest must take it carefully and throw it out of the window. But wait until the attack is past. They'll run up in waves, and then retreat," the Rev Shaw said.

He eyed the rafters which were still in position. They were not able to remove them from the sturdy centre beam and so there was still a danger of them catching alight. However, such an eventuality would not constitute any real danger to the people within the building. The worst of it was that the women could not see what was happening. They could clearly hear the natives chanting and stamping their feet. This was some distance off but imparted a fearful sense of foreboding. It was almost a relief when the noise became closer. But there was no one who was not horribly scared when the first attack came, the whistling noise of the assegais and burning sticks suddenly obliterated by the ragged gunfire as the invaders came into the firing line. The settler men shouted out, more to keep their own spirits up than anything else. Then there was silence as the attackers withdrew to regroup, dragging their dead and wounded back with them.

One of the women in the church, fearing that the ensuing silence meant that the menfolk had been overrun and slaughtered, let out a scream that chilled the blood. Immediately half a dozen others took up the cry and there was a fearful uproar in the little church. Even the Rev Shaw seemed unable to control himself. Anna Maria tried to quieten the panic-stricken women but this time it seemed to no avail. It was only when she started singing as loudly as she could that the wailing gradually changed to singing, Anna Maria calling out the words of hymns while the others tried to keep the tune. The noise from the church drowned the sounds of the second attack. This time there were two waves in quick succession --- the first being the assegai throwers who concentrated on the fortifications of the defenders, and the second with their burning sticks which they threw with great aptitude at the stone building behind the first line of resistance. The clattering of a dozen fiery brands and the setting alight of clothes and hair within the church caused a fresh outburst of panic and screaming. But several of the women heeded Anna Maria's earlier instruction, firmly grasped the sticks and threw them out of a window or over the top of the walls.

"Now listen to me. Gather here, next to the inner wall. You'll be safe. And do keep quiet," Anna Maria implored them.

The next wave of arson was not nearly so terrifying. They were able to cope with the flames without injury or panic. And they were heartened now by the deep roars of their men signalling another success in repelling the invaders.

The attacks became less severe, and the time between each attack became greater. Finally, not long before dawn there was complete silence. Miles Bowler ordered the men to stay at their posts, however, until the first light of day showed that the plain in front of them was deserted. Then he and George Sewell carefully reconnoitred the area before returning to the beleaguered church to comfort their women. The Rev Shaw and Anna Maria were already attending to those who had incurred wounds --- mainly burns and assegai lacerations. Then of course there was Hawk 's stab wound and feverous condition which had become more acute during the night.

Sewell arranged for a pony trap to convey the Bowler family to Grahamstown. Some of the settler families followed in their own transport while those who lived nearby returned to their homesteads to recover from their ordeal. Anna Maria remembered little of their journey to the larger town. She was taken straightaway to the hospital where the nurses made available a little a room adjoining the ward and Anna Maria moved in to be near Guy. He seemed to be making good progress but in the space of two days, he suddenly deteriorated. "It's poison," the sisters told her. "Poison of the blood. There's nothing we can do."

Anna Maria bathed his stomach and chest. The wound down by his groin was now dark and festering. Thin blue lines radiated upwards from it on his pathetically thin body. All that day she stayed at his bedside. Before nightfall, he died, slipping away quietly.

Anna Maria and the old Jew

The first months after the death of Guy Hawk were difficult. Anna Maria was uncertain of the future. She and the children moved to Iron Crown even though there was no suitable habitation there. She could not bear to spend time at Narrowdale which was redolent with the memories of her husband. Jocelyn was at school in Grahamstown and returned for the holidays. Jeremiah was slowly building up the sheep herd on the farm. And they had hired out Narrowdale to neighbouring farmers in the Bathurst district. And Fred was engrossed in his ostrich venture.

Then Anna Maria decided on a course of action. She sent the Hawk wagon, the one that had transported them to safety at the time of the invasion, to Algoa Bay in the charge of Aaron Hertz, an itinerant trader or smous to use the Boer name. Jeremiah counselled her against the move, cautioning her that the old man could well disappear with the valuable vehicle --- or perhaps lose it in an ambush. But Anna Maria disregarded these words. She looked to the only opportunity to build up some sort of capital for the family, that of trading. And trading also with the black tribes across the frontier. She was far-sighted in her resolve, if a little light-headed at considering the risks attached to the enterprise.

She felt it was unwise for the family to pin their hopes altogether on sheep but was unsure what to do until Aaron arrived on the scene. Then the plan developed. Aaron Hertz was to be her partner, Anna Maria said to herself. He had a lifetime of commerce behind him. The old man was from Russia and had come out on a tea clipper with enough to start a very modest itinerant trading business. He had no pretensions, no high-flown ideas. Anna Maria trusted him from the first time she met him. He was offering to supply moleskin and muslin and agreed to exchange these goods for some books when she told him she had no money. He had a small Cape cart, rickety and insubstantial. His only horse was in a like condition, rheumy and miserable. Anna Maria offered Aaron Hertz accommodation for the night, and the wild plan she hatched that evening gradually assumed respectability as she refined her thoughts during her sleepless hours.

Aaron Hertz's ability to play the violin, she heard him bowing the delicate strains of Debussy late into the night, convinced her that he was a man of culture and integrity. She had second thoughts in the morning. He was small, ugly, hunched up. His attire was decrepit and smelly, a black jacket threadbare at the elbows and cuffs. He could hardly speak English. His voice had a dreadful whine to it.

But she strengthened her resolve. It's an opportunity I should not forego, she told herself. And after some agonisingly slow discussion, bolstered with sign language and reference to a map, the deal was struck. He would take the Hawk wagon and a span of her finest oxen to Algoa Bay. He was to purchase as many wire beads and cotton goods as Anna Maria's agent would give credit for. Here was her letter to him. Old Kleinbooi would accompany him, and his little nephew Jannie to lead the tou. Three months should be sufficient --- four to be on the safe side --- for the return trip and a tour of the Boer settlements and the native kraals in the tribal areas that bordered the farms.

"Trade with the kaffirs?" Jeremiah asked scornfully. "What about the memory of your husband? He would surely turn in his grave."

"Nonsense." She dismissed that sort of talk. "The British built their empire on trade. We must have economic interdependence with the black tribes across the frontier."

But her arguments carried little conviction with Jeremiah. Naive, he said. No Kaffirs, no Kaffir wars, was his philosophy. But still he noted what she said. He admired her spirit and her honesty. Of course it was hard to make such a choice. She was just as bitter with anguish as he was. Reason and moderation did not come easily to anyone in a country brutalised by racial antagonism if not outright war.

"Nothing short of downright punishment of their whole race and country will bring them to their senses," Jeremiah said defiantly.

"Jeremiah," his mother sighed. "Sometimes I think you just say these things to antagonise me." She smiled at him. He had, after all, filled the void in the family's life in the past five years. He assumed a calm authority soon after the death of his father. He took control of all matters relating to the farming operations. Not only did he display unceasing energy and effort, as though he were driven by an inner power, but also a practical knowledge that his mother could hardly believe.

When Aaron Hertz finally returned from Algoa Bay on the last leg of his trading trip Jeremiah was the first to acknowledge that his initial reservations were probably unfounded, and these misgivings were forgotten. "Ve celebrate," Aaron announced. He proudly displayed flour, raisins, a leg of mutton, a bottle of vinegar. He noted Anna Maria's look of concern. "No," he told her. "My gift to you. Our trade goods, they are here." And he showed her the boxes of merchandise neatly stacked in the wagon.

Trading it was then. Aaron set off again the next week and the pattern was established. Two or three months away bartering, selling of little manufactured items that were in great demand and returning once more with his gains --- cattle, animal skins and horns, some money, brilliant birds feathers, one or two ostrich eggs, snake skins and a variety of carved wooden artefacts. Aaron was never molested. Even during times when he encountered warriors on the march, he was not threatened or sent away. His was a familiar presence, his business was understood and accepted. There was a chance that the womenfolk would have complained had their "shopping" been interfered with.

The Hawk wagon, a welcome sight to Anna Maria when it returned, was spotted several miles away. It looked like a ship coming into harbour, its white sail cloth catching the sun, the twelve oxen straining at the yokes, already smelling the familiar odours of home, hardly needing to be urged by the tawny little Hottentot, wearing but little attire at all, not ceasing in his unintelligible jargon of encouragement, incessantly cracking his huge whip. Aaron walked behind the wagon, not because he was particularly fond of the exercise but because he could not withstand the terrible jolting from the rough and rocky tracks the wagon traversed. In many places, so precipitous and uneven was the terrain it was highly dangerous to remain in the wagon and the unwary passenger might be knocked about and bruised, even suffering a broken neck.

Jocelyn, home from school, raced out across the open plain late one afternoon to meet Uncle Aaron and to search his pockets for the little treats he brought ---brightly coloured pebbles, dolls made from mealie cobs and dressed in pretty scraps of cloth, model oxen made from clay.

Anna Maria carefully went through the huge wooden kists mounted firmly in the wagon, sorting out the bartered goods, evaluating, appraising, seldom discarding but occasionally clucking her disapproval. She noted the items in a little black book and Aaron checked her totals, nodding his agreement. He produced the invoices and receipts from their Algoa Bay agent whose own trading repertoire had increased considerably with the unusual items brought back from the interior.

At the end of the month, the old Jew came to the family with two requests. One was that he wanted to establish a permanent trading store some miles from the homestead on a small piece of Iron Crown land. He wanted to cut down on the travelling to about two or three months a year. Also he now had enough money to send back for his family to join him.

"I wish you to teach me to speak English like you do."

"Of course, I will teach you whatever I can," Anna Maria said. They shook hands." It's a deal. I'll teach you to speak English like a native."

The old man shook his head vigorously. "I wish to speak it like you do, not like a Hotnot." Anna Marie laughed and told him that he meant a native of England. This was a silly term to use to a Russian Jew stumbling with his first English phrases. But the old man was quick to learn. "Yes, we both speak like natives very soon."

Anna Maria summoned her sons to meet her after breakfast. The previous evening she had heard them arguing, their voices rising to shouts. She had tried for some months to ignore the fact that the relationship between them was becoming more and more strained. First, there was the question of rivalry. Jeremiah had, as he had promised to do, established the finest sheep farm in the area. He was understandably jealous when Fred scored a spectacular success with his ostrich venture. But he had never been anything but courteous and unobtrusive. Then there was the question of Netta and the new baby. The boy, whom they had christened Wilmot, was unmistakably like Fred. His skin was fair, his hair blond. Anna Maria knew that the two men could not continue living on the same farm. Fred had already moved out of the main house to his own quarters built onto the old summer pavilion. But even this proximity was too close. And now, Fred had acted stupidly and endangered the very existence of Iron Crown through his borrowings. It was best to have it all out in the open, once and for all.

Anna Maria poured tea for her sons and herself. "Well, Fred. Perhaps you should tell us exactly where you stand in your ostrich venture."

Fred let his head drop between his hands. It was almost as if he wanted to blot out the reality. All three knew that the final act in the drama of the ostrich slump was being played out. Fred looked at his mother who was waiting calmly for hm to speak.

"A month ago I borrowed a substantial amount for the purchase of another 500 ostriches. I paid for the birds by bankers draft just a week before the crash."

"Have you taken delivery of them?"

"No. The birds are quite valueless under the new circumstances. It would only incur additional expenditure for no purpose."

"May I ask, from whom did you borrow the money?"

"Aaron Hertz."

"And what did you give him as security?"

"I signed a personal surety."

"Ha. That means nothing." This was Jeremiah speaking. "Fred's personal surety, without my backing is as worthless as those 500 ostrich chicks. Hertz can sing for his money."

Anna Maria rapped the table with her hand. "Jeremiah! Fred is a Hawk. His surety has the same worth as one signed by you or by me."

"Then how, may I ask, is he going to honour it?"

"The family will honour it," Anna Maria said firmly.

"Have you got any assets at all?" Jeremiah asked his brother. "You have ploughed everything into more stock, not so? You have no reserves against a bad year? You call yourself a farmer?"

"Fred, please will you call Mr Hertz to see me. Then I would be obliged if both of you could remain in your quarters while we discuss this situation," Anna Maria said. Fred left the room. Jeremiah paused at the door.

"Well, mother. Things are in a bit of a mess, thanks to your blue-eyed boy." Anna Maria held up her hand as her elder son started protesting.

"We cannot talk about that now," Anna Maria said. "First I must talk to Mr Hertz, alone. Then we will discuss the other matters."

Anna Maria and Aaron Hertz spent the whole afternoon in her study. Tea was called for from time to time, and some sandwiches from the kitchen. Finally the two brothers were once more sent for.

"Aaron and I have reached agreement on the ownership and management of Iron Crown. Some of our decisions have been arrived at after long and painful discussion and I now ask you both to accept what I am going to say in the knowledge that it is best for the family as a whole." Anna Maria looked at Aaron Hertz who nodded at her and smiled.

"Aaron will henceforth assume overall responsibility for Iron Crown." Jeremiah gasped in disbelief. Anna Maria looked at him sympathetically and went on. "Iron Crown will continue its main business as a producer of high quality wool and we will of course terminate all ostrich activities.

"We will introduce a new element into the business of Iron Crown in the form of meat production and processing. Aaron will attend to the setting up of an abattoir and the other facilities he requires.

"Fred, I am afraid that you will have to leave Iron Crown altogether. Of course, in his new position, Aaron will occupy the main homestead here at Iron Crown. I will continue to occupy my quarters here and will continue to devote my energies to the gardens. I am rather tired now and I would be obliged if we could leave all further discussion until the morning. Thank you."

Fred's Trek to the Delta

Fred remembered that one of father's regrets was that he had been unable to pursue the call of the bush. The idea of funding an expedition to explore the Kalahari and Lake Ngami had appealed to him. The country north of the Orange, and indeed up to the Limpopo attracted big game hunters. Here the plains were stocked with immense herds of blue wildebeest and zebra whilst in the woodlands roamed large game such as buffalo, giraffe, sable and roan antelope, tsessebe, kudu and waterbuck. In the years to come, Frederick Courtney Selous, a legendary figure in the annals of exploration and hunting, and a companion to Theodore Roosevelt on safaris to several continents of the world, was to be a regular visitor here.

Now was the opportunity for Fred to familiarise himself with the art of hunting which he had read so much about. Although in the past he had exhibited some diffidence towards the more manly activities, this would be an opportunity to change that without necessarily cultivating the killer instinct. Secretly Anna Maria felt that the shooting of wild life was sordid and uncivilised. But she agreed that Fred should undertake such an excursion and that this would give him a new perspective on things. Anna Maria took Fred aside. "Your father believes that hunting is the pursuit of a gentleman. Don't ever do anything to disprove his premise," she said.

Fred was very serious about the logistics of the trip. He was determined to ensure that he would have every facility to enable him to bring back trophies, perhaps even quantities of ivory. The outfit he chose comprised two wagons, one a large ox-wagon drawn by a span of 16 oxen, and the other a small, light spring wagon drawn by 14 donkeys. The latter transport was required when they entered the tsetse fly country, donkeys being immune to the deadly bite of these insects. The guns he selected were an American 500 Express Winchester, a Martini Henry and a "Colonial" gun, its left barrel being a 500 bore rifle and the right a smooth bore for the pursuit of feathered game. A dozen Hottentot were recruited. One claimed to have knowledge of the area to which they were headed.

They set off on the journey. First their route lay north-westwards through the districts of Somerset, Graaff-Reinet and Beaufort. Then, after they crossed the Zak River, they swung northwards along the great highway to the interior used by Burchell and John Campbell. It was already known to travellers as the "Missionary Road" with Moffat and later Livingstone using it as the first leg of their explorations into central Africa.

Fred's expedition coincided with the start of the great movement of Dutch farmers in search of "fresh fields and pastures new" by which the primitive Boer element was to be thinly diffused throughout the greater part of Southern Africa. The Boer trekkers held a northward course until they had crossed the "Great River" and thence eastward to what was to become Natal.

At one of the kraals along the road, they came across one of the Batlapen tribe who had worked for Robert Moffat at Kuruman for most of his adult life. He was now an old man and had retired to his tribal village. He was happy to see them and to give them his blessings. There was nothing in his interpretation of the good Book which forbade hunting. Also there was often a bounty in the form of meat and skins. "You need a good guide," he told Fred. He said his name was Salvation, and he spoke excellent English.

The travellers were not to know their extreme good fortune. The recent rains, perhaps the most bountiful in seven years, had resulted in the arid ground being covered with a fine carpet of soft green grass. There were pools of water for man and beast to slake their thirst. At the first large pool of rainwater they encountered after a week of tedious plodding through the sandy track, those oxen which were not in harness, raced forward and entered the water until they were up to their necks. Then they started drawing in long refreshing mouthfuls until their sides, which were formerly collapsed, distended as if they would burst.

Fred had the time of his life. He alternated between riding with the guides several miles ahead of the wagons and accompanying the Hottentot youth who taught him to handle the slow-moving placid oxen. In the afternoons when they had outspanned the animals, Fred spent his time in entering information in his journal and studying the surrounding countryside. He had brought a wide selection of writings by earlier travellers. One in particular, Farini[4], was most apposite in that he had been along this very route. He propped up the book and began reading aloud:

For the past four days we have traversed undulating country looking almost like an English corn district, covered as it is with a golden crop of Bushman grass which is now ripening and is almost equal to oats as fodder for the horses and cattle. We soon left the more fertile, better watered and more thickly peopled region of the Colony. Our northerly route traversed less inhabited and arid wastes which appear to suffer from a deficiency of surface water for the greater part of the year. The soil has a good coverage of pasturage (coarse tall grass) and dense thickets of scrub (thorny Acacia). We also notice many large forest trees including one called a Baobab, a truly amazing specimen which looks remarkably like a giant turnip growing high up in the ground. Then we entered the desert where the sands are disposed in vast ridges from a few feet to several hundred feet high, often over 50 miles wide and running in straight lines for hundreds of miles. Although traversed by tracks known to Bushmen, they presented a formidable barrier to us and it was only after several months of incredible hardship that we were able to reach our destination.

Now Fred's party was approaching the same destination, the game-rich territory around the delta. They set up camp several days later on a hot midday, under some spreading trees near the river, and the cattle were outspanned from the yokes. Then turmoil ensued. At first, Fred thought they had disturbed a swarm of bees. Several of the cattle lowed and tossed their heads in confusion. Then the noise rose to a crescendo and the beasts bucked and snorted. One large ox broke out of the rough thorn enclosure that had been set up. In an instant the others followed, moaning and bellowing. Dust was flung up, their possessions trampled and the animals galloped away. It was the tsetse fly, and the travellers were soon to learn the dreadful agony of their bites. They began slapping and flicking at the large insects that seemed impervious to their efforts.

"Quick," Salvation shouted. "Get away from the trees." They raced out from under the boughs and found that the flies began to desist from their attack. What relief. Their arms and legs were already showing the angry red bumps and weals that characterised the bite of these flies. Their servants had

---

4   (With acknowledgement to GA Farini's "Through the Kalahari Desert")

followed their example and after the party had regained some composure, a team was sent out to recover the fleeing cattle. They managed to recover their stock and after inspanning the wagons again, headed for the higher ground away from the water line.

They set off at first light the next day, Fred on horseback and the guide and bearers on foot. They left the oxen and the large wagon at the kraal. In due course it would be loaded with their skins and trophies for the return trip. Fred despatched two of the Hottentots with the donkey-drawn spring wagon on a course indicated by their guide which would skirt the tsetse fly territory in an easterly direction. In the midday heat the last place to seek refuge was in the shade of a tree. For there were the dreaded fly which would drop on their unwary hosts, animals and humans alike and inflict the most stinging bites on their skins. Sleeping sickness was the terrible risk in this dice with death and only the foolhardy would willingly expose himself and his horses to this possibility.

However, if the hunters kept to the grassy plains and lush valleys during the day, and returned to the safety of their camp on the higher ground at night, they might avoid the fly. After they had arrived in the hunting grounds, a suitable site was selected for the base camp, and it was from this point that they set out early each morning for hunting. After a few days the donkey wagon made the rendezvous with the hunting party as planned. Their camp could only be reached by crossing a deep ravine leading into the river and this they traversed by tying a large mimosa tree behind the wagon to prevent it from overrunning the donkeys. Each wheel was secured firmly with a wooden block-brake and *riems* were tied to the wagon sides and looped around trees on the bank.

Shooting for trophies and for the pot was to be the order of the day. But a fine skin was also an attraction. The wagon was to be heavily loaded with skins and trophy horns and sent back to the kraal to transfer its cargo to the larger wagon thence to return for its next load.

"We have finally arrived at our destination," Fred recorded several days after their unnerving experience with the tsetse fly. "This is the area in which I will set up a permanent camp and from here we will venture out on our excursions."

He had entered into what any man would call a sportsman's paradise. At one point, standing on a high ridge, they were able to count no less than 64 troops of wildebeest, each troop containing between 50 and 100 of these ungainly looking antelope, their shaggy heads tossing as they loped along, their imbalance caused by hindquarters which seemed to belong to another animal species so small and wasted were they in comparison with the forelegs. While they were quietly observing this scene, a bull giraffe, which was grazing several hundred yards away, made its meandering progress towards them. The huge creature finally stopped some 10 yards away and turned broadside. Salvation nudged Fred and passed him the Martini Henry rifle. Fred, holding his breath and not moving his position, raised the rifle and shot the animal dead with a single bullet. When he measured it, he found it was over 6 metres feet from hoof to tip of nose.

Fred was determined to shoot a lion. There is a tremendous difference between hunting antelope and lion. The former can be killed by stalking it carefully until within shooting range and then selecting the most vulnerable spot. The risk one takes is that by stepping on a twig or getting on the wrong side of the wind one loses the chance of a kill. The antelope runs away. But the lion will attack its predator. Even if it is wounded it will not flee. It will attempt to charge its assailant and nothing will divert it from achieving its objective save disablement and death. What wonderful courage.

Fred wrote in his journal:

I and the guide approached to within 30 yards of the carcase of a buck we had left as a trap. Suddenly a lioness bounded out of the rushes on the bank of a dry river bed, standing with her flank towards us and her head turned round. I was able to place an express bullet in the fleshy part of her left hind leg. She uttered a most savage and vicious roar. Then, with great precision, I broke her other leg with my next shot. And then I hit her with a charge of buckshot doing her no further damage. She started bounding round and round growling and roaring, gnashing her teeth and clawing with her massive paws at an imaginary foe on her back. When she saw us, she charged. Hindered by her terrible wounds she was unable to move with her accustomed speed and she was finally brought to earth by another volley of shots, one of which was fired by the old guide Salvation, him having been provided with your old Tower musket. The lioness proved to be a very fine specimen, measuring over nine feet in length from nose to tip of tail.

What was equally remarkable was the behaviour of Salvation afterwards. I told him for a joke that the very large hole in the skin was his bullet hole. He became wild with excitement, and rushed frantically around the fallen lioness with his gun in one hand and his assegai in the other. He uttered the wildest of shrieks and bounded from side to side in the most active of manner, stabbing imaginary foes at each bound.

"Shouting and jabbering in his own phrases, he stated what a mighty hunter he was and what game he had slaughtered and that lions were but dust under his feet, until he had quite exhausted himself.

"I laughed at his antics which had been a wonderful diversion, almost a salvation, from the grim slaughter of a splendid animal.

One afternoon Fred and Salvation came across a troop of buffalo which were extremely wild. They wheeled and ran off and in an instant Fred fired. A buffalo cow skidded and tumbled in the dust before springing to her feet again and following the herd. "I will have to finish her off," Fred told his guide. You had better come with me." They set off at a brisk pace and after a while they came across the wounded animal lying under a tree. Fred cautiously approached the stricken beast. Salvation covered his ears with his hands as his friend fired at the animal. There was a puff of dust and the animal jerked its body. "Here, reload for me please Salvation. I must not take my eyes off her."

Fred thrust the musket into his guide's hands and at that very moment the buffalo scrambled to its feet and made a mock charge. Then it stood still, head lowered, its rasping breath clearly audible. Fred instinctively grabbed the gun back not realising that it had already been loaded. run back a few paces before he could check himself. What happened next was to haunt Salvation for the rest of his life. Why he did not tell Fred that yes, he had already loaded the weapon, he could not say. The fact was that he didn't say anything. He could not explain it. He watched mesmerised as Fred carefully loaded it again keeping the snorting buffalo in his sight. When he was ready, he walked slowly towards the beast which immediately made as if to charge him. Then he fired. There was a tremendous explosion and the musket disintegrated, tearing the thumb and half the index finger off Fred's right hand.

He fell to the ground, moaning and sobbing uncontrollably. The wounded hand was a mass of bloody pulp and he ripped off his shirt and wrapped it around the torn flesh, whimpering as he did so. Salvation made him as comfortable as he could and then ran as fast as he could back to the camp. The servants were summoned and a litter was constructed out of branches. He guided them back to where Fred was waiting and he was carried to the camp.

"What do we do," Fred asked Salvation. He was still breathless and panic-stricken.

"It will be two three days before the wagon he come back. We wait."

Salvation carefully bound the damaged hand and produced a strip of bark which he said had curative properties. He gave Fred a draught of brandy and helped him to his bed.

They packed up their temporary camp, inspanned the wagons and set off for the mission, arriving three days after the hunting accident. Fred's hand was festering badly and he was worried that it would need to be amputated.

The mission station consisted of huts clustered around a large hall, all the buildings neatly whitewashed and surrounded by vegetable and flower gardens behind thorn enclosures. Salvation led the mule cart to a simple two-roomed house. Fred observed that the fields were tilled in a desultory manner and the cattle were scrubby and thin. The community of several hundred families dwelt in huts spread out around the valley. They appeared to live in peace if not in industrious occupation. Vater Friedrich, for that was the missionary's name, greeted the visitors courteously. Salvation told him in a quiet voice that the man needed medical attention. They both looked at Fred, sitting uncomfortably on a litter in the cart. Salvation pulled back the blanket. The missionary clucked in sympathy as he inspected Fred's wounded hand.

"I wish we had the proper facilities here that are required. It is something that I have been asking our Mission Society for but so far to no avail. We will do all we can. But you must understand that I am not trained in medicine. Let me call the lady who looks after the afflicted."

He called out and a tall woman of striking beauty appeared. Fred regarded her delicate wrists and ankles, and her large brown eyes. "Riba, see what you can do for the poor man. I am sure with a little rest he'll be all right. She will show you to a room where you can sleep."

Salvation helped Riba take Hawk to a nearby hut. They laid him out on a bed, pulled off his boots and covered him with a light blanket. Later Riba returned with a bowl, some bottles of disinfectant and bandages. Hawk groaned as she stripped the dressing on his hand and applied her medications.

Fred felt that the missionary really wanted them to stay because he needed company. He certainly did not need any encouragement to talk about the mission. Vater Friedrich appeared to Fred to be prematurely old. He was, he told them, no longer racked with anxiety whether the powerful message of the Gospel was being properly received by the community at the mission.

"I was a great fighter for the gospel to start with," Vater Friedrich said with a humble laugh. "I think I have lost some of my fire. No matter. It is about time for our midday meal. You must share it with us."

Vater Friedrich led the way to the dining room where a group of men and women were already assembled. "Now let me introduce you to the brothers and sisters of the mission who also sing in the choir--- like angels." The priest said grace and they sat down at the table. Fred admired the craftsmanship of its carving and the smoothness of its wood.

"This is made from the tree of life," Riba told him, at the same time casting a shy glance at the missionary. "The reverend father does not like me to repeat this legend, but among the natives there is a superstition that the wood of this tree should never be used as firewood, otherwise all the cows will only produce bull calves." She laughed and looked again at the priest. This time he returned her gaze. "It's not true of course, but if they believe it, then it is."

Riba spent many hours with Fred while he was recovering. She sat by the bed and held his sound hand. In the afternoons he insisted on sitting in a chair at the window.

With the help of a craftsman at the mission, Fred fashioned a partial mitten out of leather which fitted snugly over the hand, with the thumb and finger sockets plugged with wool.

He became adept at manipulating the hand and before long could even manage to write in his journal again. He tried to comfort himself. "Not everyone is born to hunt. You can pursue your other interests." And so Fred elected to spend most of his time at the camp, pressing flowers and collecting butterflies which he wanted to take back to Jocelyn. He also busied himself making sketches of the scenery, including various type of antelope and other game.

At last it was time to return to the farm. Vater Friedrich came to bid him farewell.

"I was a great fighter for the gospel to start with," Vater Friedrich said with a humble laugh. "I think I have lost some of my fire. No matter. Is it so bad for a man that he is no longer racked with anxiety whether the powerful message of the Gospel was being properly received by the community at the mission?"

Marshall's Evasion

"The first time I met Marshall", Clea started, was while he was still a schoolboy. I was staying with his parents for a weekend together with my mother who had just come out from Europe for a visit. He was so vulnerable..." her voice trailed off. Could she ever tell anyone the real story? God, she was a lot younger then too.......

"Come on, Clea. Let's have some sport. We're bound to find some guinea fowl down at the river, perhaps even a duiker." Marshall was holding the point two- two rifle he had taken from the main house the previous evening. He stood at Clea's window at dawn, according to the arrangement they had made. Clea, who was suspicious of fire-arms in general, was not enthusiastic, but being the guest, agreed. She dressed quickly and joined him on the terrace. They made their way across the spacious lawns and along a path. As they approached the river, Marshall motioned to Clea to stay back. He crept through the bush to the water's edge. The pool was quiet and deserted. With the dew as yet untouched by the morning sun, Marshall's progress through the undergrowth was clearly marked.

Suddenly, from the other side of the river, came an agitated cackling and a flock of guinea fowl raised their fat bodies on whirring wings and disappeared into some trees further down. Marshall cursed when he saw the cause of the disturbance --- a young black girl coming down to the water with a container poised delicately on her dark head. With a horrified gasp, Clea saw Marshall take careful aim at the girl and the quiet morning reverberated to that single flat crack of the rifle. Birds called. At the nearby native kraal, dogs barked. And the girl fell in a heap without a sound.

"Oh, God. Let's get out of here." Marshall turned and rushed past Clea, heading for a plantation of eucalyptus. Clea, almost paralysed with fear, stood rooted.

"Come on, come ON," she heard Marshall shout. With her heart pounding, she turned to follow, suppressing a yell of panic which hovered at the back of her throat. She caught up with Marshall when he stopped amongst the 10 year old trees. They stood facing each other, panting. Marshall was white-faced and tears were half formed in his frightened eyes.

"I tried to shoot the bloody bucket off her head. I just wanted to give her a fright."

He collapsed like a folded deck chair at the foot of a tree. "I was shooting at her water tin. I had it in my sights. She frightened the guinea fowl. I was going to give her a fright." The words came rushing out. He stared at Clea. "I wanted to give her a fright."

Clea, her breath coming in painful rasps, was unable to speak. Marshall spoke again, whimpering. "You know I was only playing the fool. I just wanted to shoot that tin off her head. For God's sake, what the hell are we going to do?"

Still Clea was silent. That moment of terror was etched on her mind. The girl had fallen in an untidy heap. She had dropped in her stride. Marshall had shot her. Marshall had killed her. He would be hanged for murder. He was a bloody silly bloody fool. He had shot someone. He had lifted his gun and shot someone walking down the path to fetch water. Why had he done it? He would be hanged. Or put in prison for the rest of his life. A little black girl. Shot.

"Clea, I didn't mean it. Oh, this bloody gun." Marshall sprang up and started sobbing. He grabbed the rifle by the tip of the barrel and swung it hard against a tree. It dropped from his hands and he picked it up again. He crashed it again and again against the thick trunk. The stock cracked, and then splintered. Still Marshall went on an on, sobbing and panting. The woodwork disintegrated. The trigger guard buckled. Marshall hit and hit. Finally he hurled the useless weapon away from him. The echoes of his outburst drifted away. The only sound was the wind, gently stirring the silver green glossy leaves of the blue gums. And the sound of Marshall's breath and the dying sobbing in his throat. Clea's heartbeats sounded loud in her ears.

"Come on, Marshall. I'll take you back home." Clea took him by the hand and led him slowly back to the house. She took him to his room, a rondavel in the garden a little way from the cottage where his parents lived. He flung himself onto his bed. He kicked off his shoes and pulled the bedclothes over him, over his fully clad body, over his head.

Clea quietly sat down on the door step. They hadn't been away for more than 30 minutes. Now, what had happened? She sat motionless. Marshall seemed asleep. A short while later one of the house servants came. He said politely in English that the master wanted to see Marshall. Marshall sat up in bed. He seemed composed. He said nothing. He pulled on his shoes and Clea followed him to the house, not knowing whether she should remain with him or not.

Colonel Hawkesworth was waiting in the lounge. He looked older than the previous evening. His well-built and neat frame was clothed in khaki trousers and a short sleeved white shirt. His arms were covered with a mat of greying hair. His eyes were cold, expressionless.

"Well, Marshall?"

"Dad, I've just got up. I've been asleep."

The older man turned to Clea, who stood stock still and said nothing. "I've been asleep," Marshall repeated. He had barely uttered these words before his father took two quick paces towards him and knocked him to the floor with a hard blow from his open hand. Marshall lay mute, his eyes showing fear, and blood slipping from the side of his mouth.

"Where is that gun, Marshall?"

Marshall got to his knees. In that ridiculous posture, as though he were about to crawl forward, he said softly, "The gun, Dad. I haven't got the gun. It's gone."

Clea winced as the man hit Marshall again, knocking him once more to the carpet. Marshall lay crying quietly. His father took a heavy knobbled walking stick from a copper stand in the corner. He stood over the prostrate boy and said quietly, "Get up."

Marshall did not move. "Get ... up." The two words were punctuated by two hard blows with the stick on the boy's buttocks. Marshall leapt to his feet with a cry of pain. He screamed as he was hit once more. Clea saw the dark stain of urine spreading on Marshall's trousers.

"And you?" The man turned to Clea. "You had something to do with it?" Clea said nothing. She had turned her back and bent slightly forward. The sudden, hard impact of the stick spread molten fingers of pain and shock, an almost unbearable tingling of agony.

"You brute. You big brute." Marshall had recovered his composure and spat out the words at his father. He stood with his back to the door and Clea knew he would run at the slightest risk of more violence. "I've broken the gun. It's useless. I've thrown it away."

"Get out now, both of you."

Clea was still haunted with the horror of the shooting. Marshall had recovered from his father's beating. He was quite cocky again, as though he had paid for his misdemeanours. It was only much later that they learnt that the black girl had fainted from shock caused by the blow of a bullet which had struck the metal rim of the container, buckling the tin and ricocheting harmlessly away.

The Party at Darryl Hawk's Place

Darryl Hawk was a very wealthy man. Ivory trader, import-exporter. Financier. Montague had little knowledge of these things at the time. But when he received an invitation to a dinner party at Darryl's house he responded with alacrity and the right amount of respect. The invitation, a personal letter signed by Darryl without any reference to the many companies of which he was chairman, was delivered by hand to the boarding house. This was obviously Clea's way of keeping in contact with him. He did not know whether she had also influenced the other letter, the one from the assistant manager of the ANS, offering him a job as a junior reporter. It made no reference to his meeting with Darryl. The invitation hadn't specified what sort of dress should be worn. "Smart casual," his landlady told him. "What do you mean, for goodness sake?" "Anything you like, as long as you don't wear a tie." She put a sort of scarf round his neck secured by a brass ring that had fallen off the curtain rail. He drove to the address, his little hired Renault somewhat out of place among the Mercs and BMs. He didn't know anyone at the party, except Darryl and Clea. Darryl was very busy greeting all his important guests and Montague entered without attracting any attention to himself. He went to the bar. He realised, too late, that he should rather have given his order to one of the waiters hovering around. He was the only guest at the bar. The barman was fully occupied trying to fulfil the orders of the white-jacketed corps. But at last he noticed Montague and immediately gave him his attention. "Sir, is there something I can get you?"

"Well, yes. I thought a glass of whisky might be nice."

"Yes, sir, any particular kind?" the barman asked.

"Whatever you have. I'm not fussy."

"If its blended whisky you like, we have Chivas or Dimple. If it's malt, there's Glen Fidditch."

"That sounds great. Give me a large Glen Fidditch."

Montague sipped the drink handed to him. He glanced around the crowd, wondering where to stand. He overheard a group of men discussing the gold price. Then he noticed Clea. She greeted him, and gave him a warm welcoming kiss. "Nice of you to come," she said. "Thank you for asking me. Why did you, by the way?"

He was emboldened by the whisky, a drink he was unused to. She smiled and greeted another guest. Montague didn't want to leave her side. To stand in the room, with a whisky in one's hand and to watch her. To gauge what her situation was. To see her in relation to an unknown factor. Darryl. He came up to Montague and shook his hand. "Good of you to come. You're the ANS man, is that right?" Montague didn't have time to explain. "You've met Clea, I believe." Darryl turned to greet someone else.

"Who else is here?" He asked Clea in a whisper. She was standing a few paces away from Darryl. She patted him on the head. "Let's look for someone interesting to talk to. Here," she beckoned a middle-aged man. "Weber, come and meet Montague Antrobus." She excused herself and went to join Darryl who was looking about him.

"Can't stand parties," Weber said, by way of opening the conversation. "Let's go into the boss's study. We can have a quiet chat there." He led the way to a panelled room which opened off the hall at the other side. The room was dominated by a huge elephant tusk, its tip and base clad in gold and suspended from a mounting by a silver chain.

"You in the hunting business?" Montague asked his companion.

"I'm a pilot. I fly people, including hunters, into the delta. But human relations is a subject of rather more interest to me than wildlife." Game in Africa was of intense fascination and interest to my people, he told Montague. But how many were concerned with the real problem of Africa?

"Which is?"

"The problem," Weber said gloomily, "is the breakdown of the tribal structure and inevitable, depressing, degrading transition towards so-called civilisation." Weber was a homespun philosopher, Montague soon realised.

In the early days, soon after he arrived from Belgium, Weber said he became interested in the relationship between civilised man and the bush, the dichotomy between sophisticated --- even decadent pleasures, and the soothing tranquillity of the "unspoiled wilderness" that descended upon one like an ether-soaked veil when one was deposited in the middle of the delta. It was like being transported back into childhood, where there was a "suspension of disbelief." Your world was once more peopled with fairies and gnomes, this time in the guise of birds and animals, and all you wanted to do was huddle figuratively on some adult's lap and listen, thumb in mouth, to the comforting words of a story, familiar perhaps in its telling, but certainly reassuring. There might be moments of scariness when a wild animal killed its prey. But then one would snuggle down in the warmth and security of the storyteller knowing that one would come to no harm.

Weber had spent many hours in the bush during his off-duty spells, waiting between flights. He had talked at length to the professional hunters and their clients, got to know the various camps and their staffs and had read many a book sitting in the still hot air. He had helped out at camps occasionally, repairing broken items, and acting as a barman. He developed a knowledge of birds just by watching the activity in the trees around the camp.

"You also learn a lot about human nature in such circumstances," he said.

"What about women?" Montague asked. It seemed that such a question was appropriate.

"The bush brings out the best in anyone --- or the worst." Weber recalled the American woman. Her husband had contracted some tropical ailment and insisted on being flown back to Johannesburg. None of the game pilots could be spared so Weber was radioed in. The man had taken medication and tranquillisers and they laid him out over the back seats of Weber's Cessna. The wife climbed into the co-pilot's seat. They hadn't been in the air long before her hand was on his thigh, casually. She looked round at her husband. He had fallen asleep. So she looked at Weber and smiled.

"What did you do?" asked Montague.

"I picked up her hand and placed it firmly back on her own lap. But apparently she misconstrued my intention."

The woman's hand had assumed a life of its own, it seemed. It had lifted the expensive khaki material of her skirt, revealing there were no panties being worn. And, to Weber's initial amazement and subsequent slow sexual arousal, she had softly and deliberately "feathered" herself, her gold-be ringed white fingers playing over her pudenda, gently opening the lips, caressing knowledgeably. Weber closed his eyes, and moved his buttocks against the seat. He looked at Montague. "She really was something." Montague saw that Weber had induced an erection merely thinking about it.

"She unzipped my trousers and then came down on me. She held me in her mouth for more than a 100 miles. What a trip."

But many of the clients of the professional hunters aggravated Weber. They regarded him as one of the camp servants. They were often the older people. "Game geriatrics," Weber called them. "Incidentally, have you ever been to the delta? Perhaps I can convince Darryl to invite you to visit the area."

"I don't know," said Montague diffidently. "Why should he?"

"Come on. I'm sure we can arrange a trip up there for you." Weber smiled. "There's quite a bit more than just the wild life. He'd want you to sort of get hooked on the bush. I think Darryl has long term motives for people like you."

Montague couldn't help thinking about Clea, of course. Was there the slightest chance that he could spend three or four days close to her? Could Weber contrive it somehow? Weber looked at him. "What's the problem?" he asked. "Money?"

"Well, yes. I can't just get away like that, either."

"What do you do? You at University?"

"I'm a journalist. With Africa News Service." Montague made it sound more important than it was.

"Well, now. I think that makes it a whole lot easier. We'll get you to handle an assignment there. Very interesting place. Interesting people. Let me speak to Darryl, I'm sure he can arrange it."

"OK" Montague said. "See what you can do." It would be fate, he said to himself. If it happens, it happens.

"What are you doing right now?" Weber asked. "Do you want to have dinner with me? Let's pull out of here."

Montague shook his head. "No, thanks. I've got to stay. Must get to know a few of the people here. Contacts, you know."

"The contacts you make at this sort of party are dangerous. People want to let their hair down."

"No, really. I'll see you again another time."

Weber gave him an enigmatic look. "So long," he said. "Don't get into any mischief."

The party was in progress in various parts of the house in varying degrees of intensity. Montague followed a curved staircase up to where a number of couples were dancing in a large room, almost in darkness. While he was standing on the landing, a woman emerged from the dance floor and glided down a corridor. She entered a room and the door closed. Almost immediately, it opened again and the woman emerged, either laughing or crying. She said to Montague "There's a couple in there, lying on the bed, half-dressed and totally unconscious."

Montague wasn't sure whether his informant wanted him to do something about it or not. He decided he should go and see, if only for his own prurient interest. He opened the door gently to be greeted by a strange scene. An exceedingly large and voluptuous girl, whom he had noticed at the bar earlier, and whom someone had described as a birthday present for the host, was trying to disengage herself from an elderly man who had appeared to have passed out. Could it be that the elderly man, overcome by feelings that he thought had deserted him some years since, resisting not at all the sudden surge of blood in his withered loins, had attempted to press his febrile penis into her soft unconscious envelope? And that, in splendid irony, his senses had deserted him just as hers had been?

The large lady, heaving herself into a sitting position, hissed at Montague: "Take this old goat off me. Who is he: Why has he passed out? What's going on?"

"Right, now, Jackie (was that her name?). That's enough of that, "Montague heard himself saying. "Get your clothes on and come with me. A nice hot bowl of soup and you'll feel strong as a ... as right as rain."

As he escorted her out of the room, giving a final tug to the back of her dress, he saw the woman informant waiting in the corridor. He whispered to her as they passed her: "For goodness sake get the man's pants back on before his wife finds him."

The fat young lady said she preferred a large brandy so they went to the bar. She was looking a little disconcerted and her face was flushed. "Do you think we could have a swim?" she asked him.

"I'm sure there's a pool nearby. Would you like me ...?"

She did not answer but led him out of a French door into the garden. She broke into a trot, at the same time loosening her dress. By the time she had covered the short distance to the pool, which was floodlit, she was completely naked. Montague hastily tugged off his own clothing and dived in after her. He managed to catch her from behind as she was nearing the steps at the other end. He cradled her large bosoms in his hands. they were surprisingly light, buoyed up by the water and it gave him a sensation of exquisite pleasure. The water shimmered in the floodlight. Jackie was lying on her back, her pubic hair floating like seaweed, crinkly and ginger coloured. He swam up to her and manoeuvred himself until their legs were intertwined. She smiled at him and with a wiggle of her body, moved behind him. She steered him to the side of the pool. He could feel the softness of her breasts on his back and her thighs' gentle pressure on his buttocks. He found himself against the pipe returning the water from the filter. A glass rod of bubbling water caressed his belly and he unconsciously lifted himself in the water until it played on his waving genitals which were being stirred about in delicious ecstasy. He reached behind him for the girl's body but she was already swimming back to the steps. Alas, she was paying no more heed to him .She continued to the steps, emerging triumphantly. She picked up her apparel and marched back into the house. Clea, who was standing at the door, handed her a large towel and gave her a friendly slap on the rump. Montague swam a few lengths of the pool, pretending he was really there of his own volition, just to get some exercise. Thus he was able to cool his ardour and he found a towel in the change room to rub down with, retrieving his clothes from the lawn and dressed. No one seemed to pay any attention and he sauntered back to the bar, now deserted by the fat lady. Was she perhaps, cleansed by the immersion in the pool, even now providing in person the birthday present that was promised to Darryl? Montague went to the television room. He had noticed the open door to this room earlier in the evening, the silent set sending out its electronic flashes to an empty space. He sat down in a leather armchair and instantly fell asleep.

Darryl found him there, much later that night. Everyone else had gone and Darryl was padding round in bare feet and a gown, emptying ashtrays, collecting glasses and turning off lights.

"Well, well, what have we here? A sleepy newshound? Come and join us in a cup of coffee in the kitchen."

Montague followed him down the corridor. He caught his breath when he saw Clea. She was standing at the refrigerator with not a stitch of clothing on her body. Without any self-consciousness she walked up to Montague and gave him a kiss on the cheek. Then she took a robe from behind the door and put it on. She went back to the refrigerator.

"I didn't have any supper tonight, I'm famished," she said conversationally. "What about a little cold sosatie?"

Birds, beasts and trees

The camp was set out under the widespread crown of a kameeldoring or camel thorn three. Montague questioned the name. "I didn't think you ever had camels in this part of the world?"

"It's actually a giraffe acacia and the archaic word for a giraffe is cameleopard. In Afrikaans, they've dropped the leopard part. To them a giraffe is a camel-horse. On the other hand, maybe the early Afrikaner trekkers thought giraffe were camels when they moved northwards into the hinterland. It's like that river in the Transvaal they called Die Nyl. They really thought they had come to the source of the Nile --- only about five thousand miles short of the real thing."

"Near Nylstroom there are two well-known trees of the kameeldoring species which are protected as a national monument. They bear a plaque which commemorates the treacherous murder of 33 Voortrekkers by Chief Makapan in 1854. They say that the leader of that particular party, Hermanus Potgieter was flayed alive while the children were bashed to death against the trunk of those two thorn trees."

"Pretty," said Montage with distaste. He fingered one of the thorns which was nearly three inches in length, almost straight, with a thick strong base.

"The missionary, Robert Moffat wrote about a lion which sprang at a giraffe and missed its hold. It fell back into the middle of a camel thorn tree and was actually impaled. It couldn't free itself and died a slow and very noisy death. But the local people find this tree very useful. The bark is burned and ground up to a very fine powder and taken for headaches. These pods," Marshall held up a thick curved pod covered with creamy grey velvety hairs, "are fed to their cows to improve their milk yield. The wood of the tree is so heavy that it cannot be cut by an axe. When it is dry, it will sink in water."

Marshall had a tame yellow-billed hornbill in his camp. It could readily be coaxed to the edge of a dead branch with a little bread. He took a blackened kettle off the embers and poured them cups of coffee. He bustled round with plates and food, setting up a simple breakfast. The hornbill fluttered at his elbow and he scattered a few cornflakes at the edge of the table. The bird pushed them around with his beak, and then flew off to its tree.

"Marshall, how can that fellow be related to the ground hornbill we saw this morning," he asked. They had come across two waddling across an open patch of veld, looking like large black turkeys but with great bulbous red wattles and enormous hooked beaks. They had watched for some time while the birds ranged the bare ground slowly, pecking at insects. The male let out a booming call which was answered by another hornbill some distance away.

"You know what the natives say? That the female call is 'I'm going, I'm going, I'm going home to my mother.'"

"If I was married to something that looked like that, I'd probably say 'Good riddance, good riddance, and don't bother to come back.'"

"The hornbills are all part of one large family," Marshall continued. "But you're right to question that. The ground hornbill is very much larger. But he has the same curved beak as this chap. And they're all rather clumsy. They fly as though their wings are too heavy, sort of floppy."

Marshall told them that all the hornbill males, except for the big ground hornbill, actually shut their womenfolk up from the time she had laid her eggs until the young were ready to fly. They nested in a hollow tree and the opening was closed up with mud except for a small hole for the beak.

"The male keeps his lady fed with insects and the odd lizard."

"Sounds like a sparse diet."

"Not at all. She gets extremely fat and in fact she loses all her wing and tail feathers. She has to learn to fly all over again, just like her babies." The camp hornbill answered the call from another, a steady "tog tog tog togge togge" rising at the end. The sun was already hot on their backs as they sat around eating breakfast.

"I remember once shooting a snake. It had invaded a social weaver's nest, you know, those birds which occupy a communal nest which is quite amazing. They construct a platform on the branch of a thorn tree and beneath this a whole lot of nest compartments are made from grass and twigs. The same nest is used for years. I've heard of one that's 100 years old and it's often occupied by other birds, especially finches. That is they try to occupy the nests but are usually driven away by the rightful owners which are extremely aggressive. Anyway, this snake --- it must have been a boomslang or Cape cobra, was hanging down with its tail curled round a branch and, with great delicacy and finesse, was sticking its head into one compartment after another, taking the eggs and young birds. The weavers were in a frenzy, flying about and diving at the snake. One flew too close and was struck by the snake. It fluttered down, dead. I shot the snake clean through the head, a lucky hit. My companion, a little black boy, cut open the body. We found 34 little snow white eggs, perfect, unbroken.

"We'll take it easy until this afternoon. Montague, there's a lookout in that Motsaudi[5] tree down by the river. Why not go over there later, or you can swim in the stream just here next to the camp. We're not allowed to, officially, but there's no problem."

Montague stood in the shadow of the Motsaudi tree. It was a monumental piece of vegetation, a good fifteen metres tall and covering an area larger than a suburban plot. He trained his field glasses on a malachite kingfisher perched low in a cluster of reeds further upstream. Its minute size was accentuated by the brilliance of its plumage --- violet-blue back, green crest, yellow breast and belly, and coral-red legs and bill. It bobbed its head several times, and then took off like a feathered arrow, flying low over the water.

Slowly, surreptitiously, he was enveloped in a cocoon of stillness and peace. The only sound was the gentle lap of the water against the gently waving reeds. And the occasional fish eagle flew low over the water, its wings almost dipping at each beat, disturbing the silence with its mournful cry. He saw the beautiful bird, its russet-coloured body and white head dominated by a proud beak. There was the sound of a blacksmith's plover, its harsh clinking notes like hammer tapping on an anvil.

Montague seemed to enter a period of extreme calmness and tranquillity. He was transported back to the days of his early childhood, and being read a story by his mother. Memories came flooding back. The hues of the animals were stronger now than he had imagined. Their profiles against the bush were sharper, their features bolder. When he observed a herd of impala, every animal's head lifted as if jerked on the same string. All eyes were fixed on the intruder and

---

5   Garcinia livingstonei

their bodies were still as statuary. Then they resumed feeding, though still alert, a white tail flicking here, a head nodding, a hind leg delicately raised.

Behind this intense liveliness was the feeling that peace prevailed, that this was the right order of things. In the bush, the game is generally not frightened, angry or in violent motion. A trio of warthog trotted on to the scene, like bit parts in a movie. They looked anxious and rather unlovely. The combination of two huge tusks, a scraggy mane and a backside that was strangely suggestive of a man with his trousers off, made the creature an object of gentle derision. One cannot take a warthog seriously.

A pied kingfisher darted by and alighted on a branch low over the water, his colouring suggestive of Indian ink flicked on a white surface. He marvelled at the intense brightness in nature, observing at the same time a lizard which looked as though someone had dropped a small pot of blue paint on its head and shoulders.

A marabou stork, said to have a hangman's eye, stood motionless at the water's edge, next to a goliath heron, slender and elegant rather than gross as the name might imply. An ungainly crocodile waddled into the water from the sandbank on which it had been enjoying the morning sun, its movements suggestive of a clockwork toy. Time went by.

Montague was content to remain where he was, letting the bush speak for itself. A bat-eared fox crouching under a bush watched him, his ears like miniature radar screens. A troop of baboons scampered out of the trees to his left. They saw him and seemed to boil over with anger, turning round to hurl insults and imprecations at him. Just as quickly, however, they reverted to scratching themselves busily, picking about in the grass with their prehensile fingers, peering under stones and rearranging their postures like spectators at a match. Children slipped from beneath their mothers' chests where they clung while there was any apparent danger.

He stood up, stretching his stiff back. He walked slowly back in the direction of the camp. An ostrich high-stepped past him. An incredibly overgrown fowl, he thought. Those huge thighs really should be covered. Then it broke into a trot. It looked like a man running with his hands in his pockets.

He came to an open lake where hundreds of flamingos stood, painted to their own reflections in the water. Their weird heads reminded him of those incredible drawings of a game of croquet in "Alice in Wonderland." The birds took off into the air, running and beating their wings at the same time. They circled round and then descended again causing a commotion like a hail storm on the surface of the lake. The white of their bodies while at rest transformed to a delicate pink as they flew up from the water, their wings revealing the colour on their inner side. A lone pelican landed awkwardly in the water, like an elderly man stepping off a moving bus.

The moon drifted out from behind a cloud bank and the surrounding veld glistened in the white light. A lion called in the distance. The party broke up early. They slept in sleeping bags on low stretcher beds around the camp fire. Marshall threw a couple of logs on to the embers.

Next morning, after a cup of coffee and a few rusks before the sun was up, Montague was taken for a drive in the Landrover. Marshall had roused him from his sleeping bag where he was rolled up against the pre-dawn chill.

Soon they came across a troop of elephants. There were three cows and four or five youngsters. Marshall pointed to the largest animal. "She's the leader of this particular family. Those two are her sisters and between them they have three calves aged about four and two babies less than a year old. There, you can see the two little ones."

Perfect miniatures, Montague thought. The whole scene had a great dignity about it. The elephants seemed to reflect calmness and confidence. There was no noise, apart from the swish of a branch being bent downwards by a purposeful trunk, and the occasional sharp crack as the branch broke. But the animals moved noiselessly. They placed their huge feet one in front of the other, seemingly without care, but without treading on bushes and tufts of grass. Those great soft looking pads seemed to absorb any sound of movement.

"Why no bulls" Montague asked quietly.

"Bulls don't run with the family," Marshall answered. "This is a strict matriarchal set-up. There's a lifelong devotion between those three cows. When one is in oestrus, they'll allow a bull in for mating, but that will only be for a short time. Maybe a few hours. Or a day. Even a week, but that's at the outside. The bull calves are driven out of the clan as soon as they reach sexual maturity. Then they'll join up with a couple of other young bulls."

Marshall let the Landrover coast along the dirt road, keeping up with the elephants as they progressed through the bush. His gaze fixed on several gliding birds high up in the sky.

"Vultures. Strangely enough, if they can't see the carcase, they seem to be stymied. They have incredible eyesight. I've shot an impala then lain on my back to watch. There are always some of those big birds on patrol way up there. You can just pick them out, little specks in the sky. Yet within minutes the first one is at the scene of the kill. They'll fold their wings and drop like a stone several thousand feet. They're hardly able to move when they land --- faces all red and puffed from the pressure of the atmosphere; like getting the bends in reverse. But they soon recover. Strut around for a minute or so then they're ready for business.

"Vultures have incredibly strong hooked beaks, ideal for ripping skin and flesh from a carcase. But their claws are weak and ill-developed. They're not able to hold their prey like an eagle or falcon. Their method of feeding is quite distinctive. With small game, they go first for the eyes. Tear them out, even while the animal is still alive. Then the mouth, the soft lips and cheeks. The leader will tear a hole in the skin of the carcase and extract the flesh by inserting his whole head and neck into the cavity. In the case of large game, including elephant, this hole will be enlarged and the birds will enter the abdominal cavity. They gorge themselves to such an extent that sometimes they cannot get out again. It's only when other scavengers --- hyenas and jackals --- have begun to demolish the carcase that they are released.

"Are there crocs in the river?" Montague asked him quietly.

"Yes, there are a couple of them living near that sandbank upstream."

Montague wondered why he hadn't told them earlier, when they went for a dip in the pool just below the camp after their afternoon walk. Marshall seemed to read his thoughts.

"It's unlikely they'll attack humans. Of course it's another matter if they hear something crashing through the water at night. That would sound like a large animal in distress. They wouldn't pass over that opportunity." Marshall sounded almost satisfied with the statement, and the effect it had on Montague.

"What about hippos," Montague asked his eyes wide.

They had been watching these ungainly animals earlier in the day, from across the river not far from the camp. They lived in proximity to a pair of crocodiles, seemingly without rancour. In fact, the hippo is possibly the most relaxed of all animals, displaying no fear of anything as he wallows in the water, disappearing for up to five minutes at a time, his nostrils sealed by a flap which is reverberated upon surfacing when a characteristic spray of water is blown in the air. Marshall had told his guests that crocodiles were tolerated as long as they did not approach too close. However, when a cow was about to give birth, their scaly neighbours were chased away.

"An adult hippo is quite capable of biting a crocodile clean in half," Marshall said. They had marvelled at the size of the beast's teeth which seemed quite out of keeping with its browsing feeding habits. The incisors and canines are used for fighting rival bulls.

"I witnessed such a fight once. It was the most terrible thing. Firstly they made the most hideous bellowing noises. Then there was the sound of their huge jaws crashing together, inflicting the most awful wounds. The water around was just a big red foaming welter of blood and gore. When you get two bulls equally matched, they fight to the death and more often than not both animals succumb. It's not surprising when you realise that those canine teeth can grow to a length of up to three feet --- like a razor sharp blade honed constantly by the movement of the jaw. Yet they are vegetarians. It takes a fair amount of green stuff to keep a two-ton hippo happy, nearly a hundred pounds of vegetation a night. They graze on the river bank like any cattle and they have been known to travel 40 kilometres in search of the right food. They are not normally aggressive towards people-unless you happen to be between them and the water. Then one is quite likely to deliver a massive bite which is inevitably fatal. They are so incensed by fire (a nice turn of the phrase which Montague marked) and if campers set up their tents too near the river they could be in danger of an attack."

A strange equilibrium exists between the three varieties of fish --- and crocodiles --- with man adding his small complication to the whole equation. Crocodiles love barbel. It's a mud fish with long whiskers or feelers on its upper lip. That's where its name comes from. Barb is the old word for a beard. People don't take to eating barbel. Apart from being very bony, the flesh is oily in texture. But crocs go for them in a big way. They also eat tiger fish but, strangely enough, not tilapia, the river bream. Apparently these fish are too fast for the crocodile. He just can't get at them. But the tiger fish does eat bream youngsters, whereas the barbel is safe from this predator because it takes refuge in the mud. It's like one of those puzzles --- who lives in the red house? The crocodile eats barbel and tiger, but cannot catch bream. The tiger eats bream but not barbel. Tribesmen like barbel but are not particularly enamoured of crocodiles. Whites like hunting crocodiles --- big commercial industry this --- and also like bream. Whose interests come first? It's a matter of balance really. When one species gets out of kilter, the whole thing falls apart.

"Reminds me of George Bernard Shaw's comment that vegetarians were really the dangerous ones in life --- of course he was a vegetarian --- while the carnivores tend to skulk away at the first sight of danger."

The Craft Shop
at the Mission Station

Manyene, known previously as Cathcart Bridge, was still only a small dusty village on the banks of a dried out sandy river. There was a pump house near the river's edge, with a three-inch suction pipe disappearing into the sand. Incredibly, with power supplied by a slow-revving Lister engine, the pump drew up clear sweet water from below the earth. It was as though the original river, fretful because of the evaporation due to the hot sun, had literally gone underground, flowing just as strongly and steadily as before. It drew its supplies from the vast sources of the delta, 70 kilometres away. The village consisted of the Government offices (a new building completely out of character with the others), a rest camp (several neat thatched rondavels, each with two beds, with folded mosquito nets hanging over them like weavers nests, built for the accommodation of visitors on official business), a couple of bars which had sprung up since the closure of the hotel (there was talk of a new hotel with a casino being planned), and a few houses occupied by district officials (they used to be white and now were black --- the officials, that is, not the houses. Although, come to think of it, the houses themselves had also come to assume something of an African demeanour --- lots of children, relatives from the country, a broken-down car, chickens, more humanity than before.)

Then, of course, there was the German mission and school. Manyene was also the headquarters of the growing shooting safari business --- both the rifle and the camera variety. The Rev Winkler was showing his visitor around the workshops when they came across a strikingly handsome young black woman, lighter in complexion than her colleagues, wearing a wrap-around garment of bright colouring, much taller than the other girls in the community.

"Itumeleng, how nice to see you," The missionary seemed genuinely pleased. How are things getting along in the world of Mammon?"

Itumeleng laughed. "Render unto Caesar ..."

The Rev Winkler turned to Montague in explanation. "I would like you to meet Tumi Malangana. Her brother, Denda Malangana is the eldest of three children born of a primary school teacher here at our mission. He is now an important figure in the community being the secretary of the local branch of the ruling political party as well as the official agent for recruiting for several of the platinum mines in the area. Kutu, the second son, was studying politics and economics at Fort Hare, until the authorities closed the university down as a result of political unrest. Now he is also an office bearer in the party but of the youth wing, whose outlook is somewhat radical in the eyes of the elder statesmen. Tumi, our favourite, is the youngest. She proved to be exceptionally bright at school and went on to become a teacher herself. Only recently, she took over our mission handicraft shop which markets carvings and curios produced by the disabled and by the crafts classes at the school. She ran it very successfully too. Until she was lured away by private enterprise."

"But I make more money for you now than ever, don't I? I'm now your best customer. And I probably have a stronger influence on your quality than before."

"Yes, I will not deny that. Now let me ask you a favour. Won't you take Mr Antrobus around your shop? I'm so sorry, I haven't introduced you. Mr Antrobus is a journalist. He's doing a story on ... what is it going to be about?"

"Wild life. The whole business of animals."

"Of course," said Tumi. "I'll be delighted."

"She knows more about this business than anyone else around here," the Rev Winkler said. "Her family's been involved in the mission for generations. I'll leave you in her good hands. Show him the sights," he told her. "Give him some inspiration from your shop."

Tumi's shop was in the mission grounds, but had a separate entrance to the main gate. There was a large sign which read "Matenga." She unlocked the front door and showed her visitor in. Montague watched her as she prepared coffee for them. Hot water from a thermos, coffee, sugar and powdered milk from tins on a shelf. Between her long skirt and small waistcoat, her smooth brown belly showed and the curve of a breast was visible when she reached up for cups on a shelf. Montague picked up a wooden bowl, dark and heavy ... he turned it over in his hands, feeling its smoothness and weight.

"What's it made from?" he asked.

Tumi giggled. "Witgat. White hole. That's the Afrikaans name. The trunks of the old trees become hollow and the rainwater collects there. The Bushmen used these trees as their watering holes. And the bark is smooth and white.

"Its other name is the shepherd's tree. It's also known as the tree of life. 'Boscia albitrunca', because of its white stem. And because it was named after Louis Bosc, a French professor of agriculture, although I think it was Burchell, the well-known naturalists, who first identified it. There was a superstition among the natives in my old part of the world," Itumeleng said, "that you should never use this tree as firewood. Otherwise all the cows would only produce bull calves. They also believed that if the berries of the witgat tree should dry out before the sorghum grain was ripe, then the harvest would be doomed to failure."

Montague was impressed by her knowledge. "Where did you learn all about this?" he asked.

"Oh, just absorbed it, you know. But I did grow up in the bush. We used to learn about these matters at our mother's knee. For instance, it was also one of the accepted customs to sing the praises of the local paramount chief from the top of the shepherd tree. Must have been a bit uncomfortable because it's shaped like an umbrella.

"Oh, I can tell you a great deal about this tree. In times of drought, the roots would be dried and crushed to make a sort of porridge. We have one famine known as the tlala ya motlhopi or "the famine of the shepherd's tree' like the 'year of the rinderpest'. Except that in our case, the tribespeople were actually able to survive by eating this porridge.

"The Afrikaners were also partial to it. Made witgatkoffie out of the roots during the depression. Mixed half and half with proper coffee, it was said to be better than the real thing. But some people said it was bad for your eyes."

She showed him a few figurines she had in the office. "We used to have a family of woodcarvers here for generations. The last of the line, his name is Mogale, perfected the use of verdite. It's a green stone. Only occurs in a few places in the country. We have good deposits near here."

"Ivory. Ever thought of having these carved in ivory?" Montague asked. Tumi cocked her head when she looked at him. "Did you discuss this with Clea? Do you know anything about ivory? Clea infuses people with the whole ivory culture." Montague acknowledged in a detached sort of way that he had indeed met her. He was very interested in learning all that he could about ivory.

"That's exactly what Clea said when she first came here. 'Ever thought of having these carved in ivory?' Of course, it depended on whether Mogale could handle ivory. He did have the grinding wheels to shape his little carvings. Ivory was like stone in some respects, I told her. In this part of the world everybody is extremely interested in ivory. We weren't too sure whether Clea knew what the game was all about. But she did. Or else she learnt very fast."

"How did Clea get involved in this business?" Montague asked.

"Darryl sent her. If you've met Clea, you must have met Darryl. It was through him that she came here in the first place, but of course she made her own way after that. She has a lot of interests in ivory. I think he wanted to set her up in the business. Of course, he didn't tell me this. I am just surmising. Nor, I gather, did he tell her. As far as we were all concerned, it was Clea's idea."

"What idea?"

"The idea of getting Mogale to use ivory for his carvings."

"Did you know Clea then?" Montague asked.

"No. We all knew Darryl of course. He had an interest in the safari business here, and used to fly in from time to time. I was still at the mission station then. Clea came down as his guest. The story was that she needed a holiday. She was said to be an artist, a designer. Darryl wanted her to get a feel for the potential of the African arts and crafts. He asked the mission people to let me show her around. We became close friends. We hatched all sorts of schemes. I think Darryl would have been a little concerned if he realised the extent to which Clea's mind was working. She told me she had her own ambitions. She wanted to build up a business enterprise of her own, based on exploiting the ivory market. I didn't tell her that Darryl had the ivory market pretty sewn up himself, as regards this part of the world."

She told Montague that she had taken Clea to the woodcarver's place the next morning. It was a simple little row of huts next to the river bank, with each hut open on one side so the visitor could see the students working on their benches. Clea was impressed by two things. One was the quality of their work. And the other was that they were all blind.

"River blindness," Tumi told her, "quite common amongst the tribe's people living near the delta. Mogale contracted the sickness while he was a small boy. But he had already shown a remarkable talent in fashioning little ornaments in clay and softwood. And the local headman realised that this was a potential money-spinner for the tribe. Actually, I'm not sure that he came to that conclusion right away. It sort of grew on him as the little boy developed his craft, and attracted the attention of all the other little boys at first, then their parents. He worked away quietly, whittling sticks and larger pieces into the most elaborate heads. He went on to groups of people, animals, and birds. Quite wonderful, really.

"River blindness doesn't have a cure, of course. It's caused by a little midge that inhabits rivers, especially rapids and waterfalls where there is a constant mist of moisture. The insects are attracted by the moisture of the eye and they settle around the eye, often without the person realising it. They lay their eggs in the eyelid itself and this hatch within a short time. Blindness comes gradually to the host. First an irritation. Then a constant suppuration. Finally a thin film grows over the eye as a protection. Then that becomes milky and vision is progressively reduced.

"Anyway, Mogale's prowess grew, and he started showing others how to work. But he insisted on one thing. The student had to be blind as well. Sighted people could always make their living in conventional ways, herding cattle, tending the crops, even migrating southwards to work on the mines."

Clea had been fascinated. She had examined the carvings. Crocodiles, hippos, elephants. Beautifully worked. And the categories of animals were identical. Quite remarkable. She had lined up four or five elephants, and one could not tell them apart.

"Amazing, isn't it?" Itumeleng had remarked. "They make about six separate species, each in three sizes. You can actually order them by catalogue and you'll get exactly what you ordered."

"How in the world does he do it?" Clea asked.

"Mogale? He's got a number of techniques which are not readily given to outsiders. My theory is that he gives his students a series of wire rings which fulfil the role of a template. But that only dictates the size. How he teaches them to fashion the features in the same way is another matter altogether."

Montague was fascinated. The story was slowly unfolding like a tapestry. The scheme which Clea had in mind took some time to develop Tumi told him. She had decided at the outset that this was one occasion when she would dispense with any assistance from Darryl. He had helped her, she would be the first to acknowledge that. But she couldn't continue to build up a huge credit with one man. She did not want to be in a position where he might one day call in the loan, so to speak. Another thing, she didn't really need anyone else. This was something between Tumi and her. of course, there were a great many obstacles to overcome. First, Mogale. They had several interviews with him, delicately skirting around the subject before getting down to business.

Yes, Mogale said, he would be happy to talk about producing carvings for the mlungu lady with a shop in the capital. Yes, he would consider other materials, if that is what the mlungu lady wanted. The same carvings, of course, just a different material. But when ivory was mentioned, Mogale seemed to switch off. His kindly understanding, wrinkled old face seemed to close down. His expression became stony. Clea spent a considerable time trying to break through this barrier. Gradually, it became apparent that the old man's fears were due to the fact the ivory was a dangerous commodity in his terms. It was usually associated with poaching and suffering. (Clea was surmising. After all, she said to herself, Mogale was an artist. He felt thus.) But more important, ivory was a commodity which could be traded in its own right. Wood, even verdite was something that everyone had access to, in some way or another. The value added to a piece of wood by Matenga's art transformed it into something completely different to what it was. It assumed a character, a personality. But ivory was already valuable. Men would steal it. How could he, Mogale, expect to acquire ivory and --- even more relevant --- store it prior to working it?

She told Montague that she had taken Clea to the woodcarver's place the next morning. It was a simple little row of huts next to the river bank, with each hut open on one side so the visitor could see the students working on their benches. Clea was impressed by two things. One was the quality of their work. And the other was that they were all blind.

Montague was able to draw some more threads into place in the tapestry that evening. He was staying over at the mission station's guest room and was surprised to find that his companion for the evening was Weber, who had flown in that afternoon. Weber was delighted to meet Montague again --- they had not seen each other since Darryl's party. Montague steered the conversation to the question of ivory carvings, and the fact that he had spent some time with Bontle discussing Clea's involvement with Mogale.

Weber chuckled. "Clea knew she was onto a good thing when she first met up with that old blind man. She was determined to get him to make ivory figurines for her, but it was a difficult job."

"What were the problems?" Montague asked.

"First of all, Clea did not want it to be known that Mongale was in fact working with ivory. There was the question of licenses and permits. Where had Mogale obtained the raw ivory, the authorities would want to know."

But it was all resolved in the end. Clea would have delivered to Mogale every day a single tusk. Mogale would work it himself and would gradually bring in the services of two or three of his best students. They would produce the same carvings in ivory as they were working on in the other materials. Every third or fourth carving would be in ivory. And that particular piece would be carefully placed in a corner, out of sight and out of touch of the casual onlooker. She would send someone down every evening to collect the finished ivory carvings. She had the ideal person. The young Itumeleng, who had recently completed her schooling, thanks in no small measure to the assistance that the mission station had provided. She would be discreet, and entirely trustworthy. The stock would be built up slowly until there was sufficient to fill a crate. And who better to take over the transportation back to Mamelode, quickly and efficiently, but Weber. He was a regular visitor to the area, perhaps twice a month. Weber was intrigues by the thought that Clea was trying to out-fox Darryl. The fact that he was paid by Darryl was quite incidental. Clea was a professional. She deserved his (Weber's) support in every way.

Clea was to pay for the ivory carvings at an agreed rate, not much below the market price. It would allow her the normal 100 per cent mark up and the carvings would be bought by tourists and locals alike, people who recognised that ivory was a commodity which escalated in value a little faster than gold, say 20 per cent per annum. He said that it was indeed a lucky chance that Clea had come to Charlie's Halt, and that she had seen some of those dreadful verdite pieces. Oh, well. These are the opportunities that come up, and it takes a resourceful person to recognise them.

"Clea said she was worried that Mogale would question the origin of the ivory she gave him for carving. Eventually she'd have to explain where it all came from. It had to sound all above board. She made up some story about a family of traders who had built the stock up over the years, buying from hunters who, in the old days could quite legitimately shoot elephant and who paid for the provisions and bearers in tusks of ivory."

She told him that she had bought some of this for herself, and some was still owned by traders who wanted to transfer their assets out of the territory, just in case, "you know."

"So that's how it started. We have been close friends and colleagues ever since, although on a lesser scale since Mogale died."

"And the ivory store?"

"That's still there. Apart from a bag or two that went to Mogale for carving."

As arranged, Tumi came to collect Montague after breakfast the next day to show him the shop. As they were walking through the mission garden, Montague asked: "What happened to Mogale?"

"He died eventually. He had built up quite a thriving little business. One of his students took over. But it wasn't the same. Standards drop. The whole thing finally broke up. Also the mission hospital came up with a remedy for river blindness. Now that was real progress. It was just a pity that the art of ivory carving amongst that particular community was one of the casualties in the process."

Tumi said that Clea had learned quite a lot from the experience. "At first she was devastated when Mogale died. She wanted to come down to take over the school. Or at least set up a proper establishment. But finally she realised that one cannot prolong something that has run its course. You have to stand back and let things go back to normal. So instead she and Darryl had decided to set up their own curio business, and they employed me to run it for them."

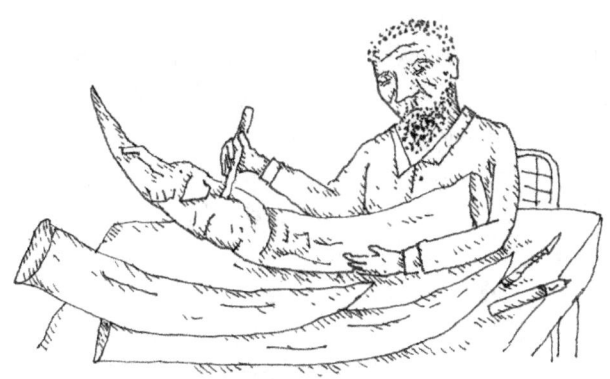

Ted and the Rhino Poachers

Ted stood at the edge of a rock face high on the Molombo mountains scanning the plains stretched out below. His task was made more difficult by a ground mist lying along the course of the river. That would soon evaporate in the morning sun, giving way to a blue-grey haze of shimmering heat. He and Montague had set off before dawn on an observation recce along the eastern border of the game park, a deserted stretch of nearly 100 miles, far from the normal tourist roads. This was the area the poachers favoured from their bases across the border, usually operating in bands of three. The poachers had refined their activities so that they were never stationery for longer than a few minutes at a time. Their strategy lay in their extreme mobility and caution. First a slow and careful search from the high ground just outside the boundary to pinpoint the presence of elephants --- a lone bull, of course, would be ideal. Then the trio would go in at a trot. Once they had disappeared into the mopane forest, there would be very little chance of them being sighted by a patrol. But equally the poachers themselves couldn't see further than a few yards ahead of them and their tracking down of the elephant depended on some very skilful ground navigation on their part.

Montague stood at Ted's elbow, using the former's powerful field glasses to sweep the sector that had been allocated to him. "I've got something," Ted whispered excitedly. "Here, give me the glasses." He focussed them on the spot he was watching, and then handed them back to Montague. "Down there in those big trees." Three of the buggers. Can you see them?"

He impatiently snatched the binoculars back after the other had failed to locate the quarry. "Come on, let's get going."

Ted started down the slope back to the Landrover at the foot of the hill. "They're downwind of the elephant, and we're downwind of them. They're not going to hear the vehicle if we keep it good and slow."

He had long since abandoned the practice of taking game guards who would sit stiffly in the rear of the vehicle, clutching their FN rifles. Guards were not at all happy at the prospect of engaging gunfire with anyone, let alone a seasoned poacher who was thoroughly trained in weaponry and who was quite determined not to be captured. He would fight to the death, and very likely it would not be his death. Ted guided the vehicle carefully along the track, picturing in his mind where the poachers were in relation to the river, and calculating where he should leave the road and start manoeuvring through the bush to cut them off. His plan was to get near enough to his quarry and then trail them on foot until the killing of the elephant had taken place. then, while the poachers were occupied in cutting out the ivory, he would apprehend them. The fact that the elephant had to be sacrificed in the process was not really of significance. Better to lose one more elephant in the hope of catching the poachers than run the risk of engaging them prematurely in an exchange of fire which could mean casualties and the chance of them being able to get away in the confusion. He quietly explained to Montague that this was going to be the course of action. They were driving slowly, the engine barely idling.

Suddenly, a burst of automatic rifle fire ripped through the stillness. It was close by, to the right of them. He signalled Montague to get out of the vehicle and follow him. He set off at a trot, crouching down, through the undergrowth. Within a few minutes they came across the scene of the shooting. A scattering of brass cartridge cases indicated that the weapon was a Chinese-made point seven six two millimetre. Ted knew that this calibre was usually sufficient to inflict death but the charge was light and thus the velocity was often too weak to allow for penetration into a vital organ of the elephant's body. He counted six shells.

The elephant had been browsing under an acacia tree not more than 50 yards away. The burst of bright blood showed that the bullets had lacerated the surface of the body. Drops of darker blood meant that certain of the shots had hit home deeply. Ted carefully followed the trail of blood. The elephant had wheeled off to the right, away from the direction of the shooting, and made off down the valley.

It was not difficult to shoot an elephant. Of all the animals in the bush, it is probably the easiest to approach as long as the wind is right. The elephant's eyesight is notoriously bad. And the first reaction from an elephant after being shot is to run away. So everything is in the favour of the hunter.

Ted put his foot in the fork of a convenient marula tree, and hoisted himself up. After waiting a few moments, he drew in his breath quickly as he observed the elephant bull hobbling across an open patch of veld, half dragging its left front leg. It paused to sweep up dust and dirt with its trunk and apply this to the wound on its shoulder. Notwithstanding its obvious distress, it was still moving strongly. He scaled down the tree again and joined Montague. "It looks as though we've got a long walk ahead of us. That fellow has a good few miles in him before he comes to his end. And the poachers are not going to give him the coup de grace because that will give their whereabouts away."

They resumed their tracking, careful not to approach too closely to the wounded elephant since this might mean over-running the poachers ahead of them. Several hours elapsed but the end came sooner than Ted had predicted. First, they heard quite clearly a human voice. Then, going forward slowly, taking advantage of all the cover they could find, they came up to a grove of trees where the last act of the drama was being played out. The elephant was using a tree to make himself into a tripod, leaning heavily on it to take the weight off its wounded foreleg and shoulder. The three poachers were squatting down watching it, not 30 yards away. The elephant's head was sinking lower and lower towards its knees. It was making a hoarse noise and breathing out great gouts of pink froth, indicating that its lung was now haemorrhaging badly.

"Can't we do anything?" asked Montague in a whisper, his mouth an inch from Ted's ear. "You can't just let it suffer like that."

Ted shook his head. "Let it be. We can't do anything now."

The breathing of the great animal became increasingly more laboured, each breath marked by a gurgling and rasping sound, while the froth turned a progressively darker red and stained the ground in front of it. At last, with a horrible choking noise, the animal staggered and fell face forward, its forelegs splayed out in front. One of the poachers, hefting a large hand axe, ran lightly up to the stricken beast and with a swift and full-bodied swing, buried the head of the weapon in the elephant's cheek, just below its eye. Montague, feeling the nausea rising in his throat, turned away from the sight of more blood and flesh. The animal made no sound, but it was still alive, and its eye dribbled and winced from this latest terrible agony.

The black man continued his butchering, laying bare another third of the tusk which is normally buried in the flesh of the face. With a few more deft strokes, he cut the tusk free from the head of the elephant and his companion came up to take hold of the tip and drag it away for rough cleaning and wrapping in a sack.

Ted was watching the man with the rifle, waiting for him to drop his guard for a moment. He sat back against a log, holding the weapon firmly in both hands. Then he got up and stretched. He laid the rifle down against the log and walked over to join the other two who were engrossed in removing the second tusk.

Ted whispered directly into Montague's ear. "Watch me. When I signal, shout as loud as you can," he mouthed. Montague nodded. Ted motioned to Montague to stay where he was, and began to creep slowly towards the discarded rifle. He made for a large tree which gave him some cover, and took him in a wide arc away from Montague, who was holding his breath in dreadful anticipation. The last few yards were traversed on tiptoe. Ted, avoiding dried twigs and leaves, finally reached the temporary safety of his hide. He looked at Montague. He raised his hand first to his lips then up in the air. As he plunged his hand down, Montague reacted by cupping his hands in front of his mouth and bellowing a loud and repeated "Hey, hey, hey, hey."

The effect of this unexpected and electrifying action on the poachers was to cause a sudden panic. The two ivory cutters jumped back from their labours, bumping into each other and almost falling over in their haste. The leader turned his head wildly round, not knowing at first what was happening and from which direction this awful noise was emanating.

Ted meanwhile had calmly walked out from behind his tree and picked up the rifle. He let loose a staccato burst of automatic fire which shattered the branches and leaves in an arc around the poachers. The three men stood in a line, frozen into immobility by the suddenness of their change in situation. Montague felt the blood hammering in his temples. His throat was hoarse from the shouting. His ears still rang with the din of the shooting at such close quarters. He walked across the open area and joined Ted.

"They just don't know what's happening," Ted said with a smile. "Scared them shitless, to use Denda's phrase." He was watching the trio closely, all the same, holding the rifle in the crook of his arm.

Montague noticed a sudden movement. "Look out," he shouted. One of the men, who had been holding an axe behind his back, suddenly hurled it at Ted, the missile describing a slow arc through the air. Ted stepped aside and the axe fell to the ground next to him. But his attention was momentarily distracted and in a wild pelting headlong rush the three men ran off, each in a different direction. Ted raised the rifle but after a second or two, dropped it again. He looked at Montague and shrugged his shoulders. "What can you do? Shoot them in the back? I'd probably miss anyway."

"You could have shot at least one of them, not so?" asked Montague.

"Never shot a man. Won't start now," said Ted.

The Ivory Heist

The ivory store at the Game Department had grown considerably over the years. In the early days, before there was any systematic culling of elephant, the only ivory to find its way into the store was the tusks of elephants that died of old age, and the occasional windfall taken from a poacher's secret hiding place uncovered by a keen eyed warden.

The location of the ivory store was moved several times over the years as the Game Department buildings were enlarged. When Ted took over as warden in charge of the northern section, the store was in the form of a large circular hut, with reinforced door and windows. Of course, all the ivory from the culled elephants went direct to the head office at the capital. The ivory store was only for tusks from animals that died of natural causes. Now Ted was retiring. The question on everyone's mind was: what's to do with the ivory.

* * *

Darryl was the first to come up with a scheme. It would not be a difficult job to remove the centre seats in the Cessna, Weber said in response to Darryl's query. The back two seats were collapsible and one could stow about 500 kilograms of ivory in the cabin. Fuel would have to be kept down to a minimum, just enough to fly out over the nearest border about 60 kilometres northward, land and return.

There were dozens of little unmanned strips in the Zipfel.

Darryl was sitting quietly in the corner. "What's that German name?"

"The zipfel. I suppose you've never heard of Count von Caprivi de Caprera de Montecuccoli? In 1890 he negotiated a treaty with England whereby, in return for a strip of territory linking what was then German South West Africa to the Zambesi River and some other territorial considerations, Germany abandoned her claims to Zanzibar." Weber was proud of his historical knowledge.

"Amazing. No consultation with the people who lived in the area?" Darryl asked.

"Of course not. But that was the least of the shortcomings. The treaty itself was based on some quaint misconceptions. It made reference to Germany getting 'access to the navigable waters of the Zambesi', the idea because one could thereby get right across the waist of the African continent to the Indian ocean. On the Zambesi!"

"That's all very interesting, Weber. But right now we're trying to decide on the best plan of action for getting ivory out of the territory,"

Three trips were all that he could do, Weber said, without arousing any suspicion. The TASP (temporary air services permit) issued by the Department of Civil Aviation covered one pilot, one aircraft and one route and Weber's route was usually into Mongu, on to the bush strip, then back to Mongu for refuelling, back to the delta strip, then home.

If he took on more fuel at Mongu than normal, or came back again to top up (which required filling in landing forms), there could conceivably be questions asked. Weber could possibly borrow fuel from one of the safari camps, but the pilots there were usually unwilling to give out any unless it was an emergency. They had too many shuttles to do, flying the professional hunters and their clients between camps in the concession area.

"It depends on how much you want to get out. Are you talking about 10 tons or more?" Weber asked.

"For this discussion, let's say 1 000 kilos.. The vital factor, of course, is speed. We have to move the stuff out in one weekend."

"In that case, I would hire one of the Tri Landers. Those big slow jobs with three engines. Especially designed for short fields and heavy lifts. Noisy, though. It had car doors on both sides of the aircraft for each row of bench seats and three engines (one on the top of the tail)."

"What is their carrying capacity?" Darryl asked.

"A thousand kilos, easily. But depending on weather conditions, the quality of the strip, and the amount of fuel you have, you could perhaps double that. Of course, the pilot would need to be a bit more bold and reckless than usual."

Weber said the best thing would be to bring in the aircraft at night, with a TASP. Possibly on a Friday. They would need to set up a small fuel depot in advance. One could fly straight into the Cape.

"Yes. I could do that. I would need a secure base at that end, but I could probably arrange that through one of the professional hunting parties."

"Right. We'll just have to get it out of the store and down here then, Weber, you can fly it out."

"That's all? No problem? You make it sound so easy."

"Well, make it easy. Sort out the logistics." Darryl always distrusted emergency plans. "Don't be ruled by crises," was one of his mottoes. "Be part of the solution, not the problem," was another.

Darryl insisted that the heist should be kept secret from Ted. So he and Weber planned the ivory heist without mentioning anything to Ted. Only Tumi was to be kept in the picture. They needed her to get hold of the key to the ivory store – and to mastermind the removal of the ivory.

The plan they evolved was quite a simple one. The driver of the big Bedford that the game department had made available to collect Ted's furniture had already made one trip. Tumi was to give him enough 'incentive' to return on the Friday afternoon for a further trip to pick up a few chairs and that old sofa which everyone knew belonged to Ted. Then, when it was time to go, the vehicle would develope a small problem with its electrical system. The driver, following Tumi's careful instructions, was to retire to the office where some refreshments awaited him, including a bottle of brandy.

Meanwhile, inside the big truck, quite unbeknown to the driver, twelve of Darryl's strong young game trackers had crept in and were biding their time. After dark, they started their labours. One sack at a time, placed on a wheelbarrow, was being carefully transported from the ivory store to the truck, each weighing about 50 kilos. They were able to load 150 sacks in the first hour and 100 in the second. Then they rested.

At midnight, the Bedford coasted quietly out of the gate. The driver was long since asleep. Only when the truck was safely out in the open did the replacement driver engage its engine and turn on the side lights.

Dawn was breaking when the truck pulled up at the airstrip homestead and there was another two hours of labour before the men collected their pay of 100 dollars a head, good money in anyone's language, especially as they were already on Darryl's payroll for the four months of the year during which he hunted.

Could they be trusted? "Not a word to anyone," he told them. "Otherwise I'll shoot you. I'll make it look like an accident," he smiled when he said this, and the men laughed. They had the greatest respect for him.

The Viper Strikes

The Gaboon viper, a highly poisonous member of the Viperidae family of snakes, has the most gorgeous colours in a pattern that extends down from its blunt triangular head to the tip of its stubby tail, a distance of some four foot. It has a quiet, almost friendly disposition. It also has the longest fangs of any known snake, over an inch in length. When the mouth is open, and the viper is about to strike, the fangs are erected by the swivel motion of the movable maxillary bone. The effect of its poison on the body is haemolytic destruction of the red corpuscles of the blood rather than the effect of other poisonous snakes which is neurotoxic.

Montague watched with horror as Clea tried to side step the snake which lay in the path. She was two or three paces in front of him. The viper flicked itself with incredible speed at Clea's bare calf. Its head seemed to caress the girl's flesh. Then it was gone in a flash of bright colour, leaving a fleck of blood to mark the spot where the fang had punctured the skin.

Clea had made a strange sound, a barely aspirated intake of breath. She staggered, and Montague quickly clasped her arms and body from behind, and eased her into a squatting position at the side of the path.

"There's a snake-bite kit in the house," Marshall cried. You hold her here."

He raced back indoors and returned within a minute. He quickly assembled the syringe, drew in a full cylinder from the rubber topped phial of antidote and injected her in the thigh, directly through her white slacks. Montague, supporting Clea's head, had lost all feeling in his arm. He was also emotionally paralysed. He watched in horror. Clea was already in a coma, her flesh damp and chilly to the touch, her face bloodless.

"Come on; let's get her inside for a few moments. Give the antidote a chance to work. Then we'll take her down to the airstrip." Marshall showed Darryl and Montague how to clasp hands to form a cradle under Clea's body. When they picked her up, her head dangled drunkenly downward. Marshall took her neck in both hands and they shuffled back across the veranda and into one of the bedrooms. They laid her down on the floor. "She'll be all right; probably just fainted from shock. Let her rest for a few minutes. Then we'll get her to the hospital at Mongu." Marshall was reassuring Darryl who was standing white faced and mute.

Montague walked outside and sat on the low wall of the veranda. So sudden, yet the sequence of events had seemed to take an age. It was like watching a drama unfold in a slow motion film. You can't stop the projector because you disagree with the ending. Oh, yes, you know what the ending will be. But you still have to sit through the performance. Champion touched Montague on the sleeve. He started, and recoiled again at the sight of the snake, its head flattened, drooped over the end of a stick.

"Very bad one, boss. He dead now."

"So I see, Champion. When one of these bites you, what happens? You die?"

The black man seemed to shake his head and nod at the same time. "When that snake bites you, you take chicken. You cut it here." He tapped himself on the chest. "Then you hold that open part on the place where the bite is. Soon the chicken, she die. First the eye close then looks like sleepy, then head falls and she die." Champion let his head loll down dramatically, his eyes closed and his mouth open. "Then you take one more chicken. You cut it and the same. She die also. Maybe third chicken. But then the person OK. The poison gone."

The frantically pumping heart of the mortally wounded bird, does it draw the poison from the bite, Montague wondered. The chest slit open with a sharp knife. What about the feathers?

"If no chickens, sometime can work with frog," Champion added.

What about the serpent's stones of the early tribes in the north? These were passed down from one generation to the next. The stone, immediately applied to the snake bite, would stick there of its own accord. After a few minutes, it would drop off, like a leech gorged with its victim's blood. The stone would be placed in a bowl of milk to purge itself of the poison. The milk would turn yellow. Then the process would be repeated. These stones, some say, were really made of bone from an elephant's skull. They would give off bubbles when thrown into water.

Weber dropped Montague and Marshall at Mongu. The young black doctor from the mission hospital was on standby at the airstrip, as per the radio request, but he could do nothing more than confirm that the medication had been correct. Then the trio took off direct to Johannesburg, three hours flight away.

Montague hitched a lift on Sunday midday from Mongu with one of the game pilots and checked into a small hotel in Hillbrow. He telephoned five private hospitals before he was able to locate Clea. No, she was not able to take calls. No, he could not visit her. She had a private ward but was under doctor's orders. Perhaps later that evening.

Montague walked to the Brenthurst. It wasn't far from his hotel. He bought some flowers in the shop downstairs. While he was paying, he saw Darryl stride past. He would have to wait. He found a bench out in the front garden which had a view of the main entrance. It was cold. A gusting wind rattled the leaves of a plane tree. Finally, the familiar tall figure emerged and walked towards the parking area. A few moments later, a Mercedes purred out into the street.

Montague asked at the desk. There was a whispered consultation between two women. One went into a back office. She returned, shaking her head. "Are you a member of the family?"

Montague shook his head.

"She had another operation this afternoon. She's still in intensive care. Perhaps you can call back tomorrow."

Montague left the flowers. He couldn't bring himself to write a note. He didn't feel anything, he said to himself. He must have prepared himself subconsciously. His return took him through a park. He sat down on a bench. He found a paperback book in his jacket pocket. He must have taken it when he left the hotel. Did he really need something to pass the time? Or was it easier to drown his thoughts in a printed page.

Back at the hotel, he watched television in the lounge. He went for a walk afterwards. Those Sunday programmes were always full of good works. He recollected an episode in the TV play. The story was about a man who had left his girl after an argument, storming out of their flat. She had gone to bed. But first she had squeezed a ribbon of toothpaste onto his brush in the bathroom. In readiness for his return later.

Montague snorted, and found himself crying. We mustn't ask ourselves, what does the world really mean. It should rather be, what do we do with our lives? And I have no desire left for superfluities, he told himself. He felt himself overwhelmed with black meaningless thoughts. The dragon of the night unsheathes his claws unseen. Where had he learned that?

The telephone woke him. A jangling, persistent ringing dragged him into consciousness from a drugged sleep. His head was full of whisky fumes. A woman reached across him and answered the phone. He voice was cracked and hoarse. "Yes, OK. Thank you. Bye."

She climbed over him with a groan and went through to the bathroom. The room was in a shambles. Montague got out of bed with some diffidence and draped a towel around his body. The woman emerged from the bathroom. She had already put on her clothes. Montague looked at her with concern. "Is there something the matter?"

"That was the porter downstairs. My boy friend's waiting. He knows I'm here with you."

Oh lord, Montague said to himself. Judy (was that her name?) works at the hotel. He chatted her up last night. They had persuaded the old boy in charge of room service to sell Montague a bottle of whisky. And they had debated with some merriment, "your room or mine." He had won.

There was a loud knocking on the door. "Judy, come out. I want to speak to you."

Montague went across to the door, opened it an inch and said. "I have the impression that she'd rather not, right now. Is there anything I can do? Would you like to leave a message with me?"

Judy called out behind him. "Oh, all right, I'm coming."

Montague looked round with surprise. She was applying make-up hurriedly. She pushed past him and he saw her take the young man by the hand. She patted Montague on the cheek, gave a cheery wave and led her man away.

Montague felt immensely relieved. He drained a half empty glass and shuddered. With a violent gesture, he tore the towel from his waist and hurled it across the room. He remembered the woman's large breasts and the fact that she had covered herself with her hands while getting into bed.

Ted's Funeral

"Whisky Hotel Kilo. Hold on runway one three."

Weber fitted the earphones and the crackling radio voice was silenced from the others. He taxied to the holding point, turned to face the morning sun, and braked. He revved the engine up to 1800 and the little aircraft strained against its leash like an eager pony pulling against the stable-hands' restraining hold. Magnetos, mixture, fuel cheques once again. Weber went through his pre-flight vital action procedure slowly and methodically. He pulled up the aerilons and gave himself one notch of flap. He turned to his passengers. "Seatbelts fastened." It was a question and an instruction. The three nodded.

Darryl turned to Montague. "In the business world, flying at this time is known as the red-eye run. Everyone's grumpy. You stand in line at the cheque in counters like a lot of zombies. You've been up since five, had no breakfast, and not even had a chance for a crap."

"What's the alternative to the red eye run?" asked Montague.

"Well, there's the gentleman's run. That leaves at mid-morning. Anyone who flies at that time has quite a different attitude to business. He can afford to spend half the day in just getting to his destination. He lands at about noon and then it's time for lunch at the other end.

"And then there's the lover's run. Six o'clock the previous evening. You tell your wife you have to be fresh for an important meeting the next day. And you get down in time to cheque in to the hotel, have a bath and then collect your girlfriend for dinner."

"Yeah. And when you get to the meeting, it looks as though you haven't slept all night which is probably true." Montague laughed.

"Then you just tell your colleagues you were on the red-eye run," smiled Darryl. He was being kind to Montague. Neither of them mentioned Clea. Weber had told Montague earlier that she was already in Mongu.

Darryl and Weber were a contrasting pair, the one tall and fair, the other small, compact and dark haired. Montague watched them during the outside inspection of the aircraft before take-off, Darryl, standing back while Weber swung the prop to circulate the oil. Weber wore a white shirt with dark epaulettes carrying the insignia of the charter company --- navy slacks and polished black shoes. Weber packed the luggage into the rear compartment, the black airport attendant passing each piece to him carefully in both hands.

It was six weeks since Montague had seen either Weber or Darryl. Darryl sported his usual casual look that was probably very elaborately effected "a laid back unstructured appearance" was a phrase that Montague read somewhere which seemed to him to sum up his companion. Khaki slacks, cream shirt, silk scarf, probably Pierre Cardin. Sneakers clad his feet the name Borg appeared somewhere discreetly and a slim Patek Philippe watch floated on his wrist.

Weber was speaking quietly into the mike. He repeated the call sign "Whisky Hotel Kilo. Runway one three. Mongu. Eight five." The six seater single engine Cessna Centurion, the Belgian pilot had told Montague, was in the same league as the larger Cessna Citation or the Grumman Gulfstream which he sometimes flew, whirling a handful of directors around the country or even overseas, men whose time and inclination did not encompass scheduled airlines, queues at counters and the inevitable delays of mass transportation.

Now Weber increased the revs again, released the handbrake and, with one hand held lightly on the stick, he guided the craft out along the runway. The needle on the speedo crept steadily up to 50 mph, then 60,70 ... and at 80 he eased the stick back. The little beast ceased its bucking and began to soar. Soon they were high and banking southwards. The aircraft, with 600 lbs of fuel in her tanks, had six hours of flying time ahead, more than ample for the 1 000 mile trip. Johannesburg dropped from sight, the taller buildings still wreathed in early morning mist. Sun glinted on the swimming pools in the suburbs. And traffic began to build up on the freeway that ringed the built up area.

"How're you going, Montague?" Weber craned round to the sole passenger in the rear of the plane.

"Fine." He was huddled in his seat. His legs were drawn up against his chest and his eyes were closed. He was nursing a wicked hangover from the flight the previous evening from Nairobi. He didn't have the head for first class where the stewards seemed to delight in plying him with free drinks.

"Don't worry, Weber is no Daedalus," Darryl said soothingly.

"Daedalus was fine. It was that pushy son of his that got into trouble," Montague retorted.

Darryl said: "I remember when a friend of mine was learning to fly. His wife would say to him every time he went off for a lesson 'Don't forget, darling, fly very low and very slow.'"

They flew at an altitude of five and a half thousand feet over dry grasslands with occasional clusters of sand acacias, the ubiquitous dryland shrubs, their sickle shaped slender pods protected against browsers by sharp straight thorns. Soon the real desert began, shimmering in the heat. Weber tapped Montague on the knee from his position in front, and pointed down. "Temperature's about 50 degrees C down there. You'd last about a day without water."

Early explorers were wondrous of the delta in the heart of the desert. Here the gradient is so slight that rivers literally run backwards at certain times of the year, where grass, reeds and papyrus are packed so tightly that the river course is diverted, where a floating mass of matter is suspended like a blanket on the water, it wobbles and shifts but is strong enough to bear the weight of a buffalo, where floodwaters dam back to form new and unchartered lakes and where fresh channels are dredged by hippos walking along the bottom.

A German explorer noted in his journal that the area was so "shut off from the outer world and difficult of access that it has retained its virgin charm. Here dead silence reigns, only now and then broken by the distant snorting of a hippopotamus ploughing its way through a reed bed, or by a hoarse cry of a fish eagle circling majestically in the air above."

Scientists have speculated that the Okavanga river was once a tributary of the Kwanda and then the Zambesi. As such, its contents swelled the mighty torrents that plunged over what were to be named the Victoria Falls. These falls, they argue, were formed by a far greater volume of water that flows over them at present.

Something must have happened to divert the flow of the Okavanga into the delta where the surrounding countryside is dead flat. It spread its waters. Perhaps a tree carried down by a flood became embedded in the shallows. Next year, sand would build up around it. Then it would collect floating debris. More sand; an island. The sluggish waters deposited drift and vegetable waste which would fill its earlier course. Foreign matter would take root and grow, like peat moss or the sudd of the Nile.

The delta only gradually unfolded itself to a succession of adventurers, many of whom were first attracted by a legendary lake which had something of the same compelling seductiveness as the treasures of King Solomon or the Queen of Sheba. David Livingstone, the famed missionary discovered this lake only to realise much later that the waters which fed it seeped from the south-eastern border of the mighty delta. Tribesmen spoke of "a country so full of rivers that no one can tell their numbers."

Livingstone realised by and by that the country up there was not "the large sandy plateau of the philosophers." The waters of the delta proved to be so clear, soft and cold that "the idea of melting snow was suggested to our minds." The lake, which bore the name Ngami, was insignificant in comparison.

A mighty delta indeed. One of the few inland drainage systems of the world into which a major river empties itself, year after year, engorged with the clear water from the up-country highlands, flooding hundreds of square miles and providing sanctuary and succour to countless fish, water birds and animals. But ---until quite recently --- not man, except for the chance visitor or nomad. For the delta is home to the scaly, slap-resistant, determined and ubiquitous tsetse fly, carrier of the dreaded sleeping sickness. One of the four great plagues of Africa --- the others are hook-worm, bilharzia and malaria --- this sickness keeps all but the

intrepid or unwary at a respectful distance. An infected bite from a tsetse fly brings as the first indication that all is not well, an ulcerated sore around the wound. Then swollen glands, a headache, an ague that freezes the bones, a racking fever, cold shivers, nausea, and mental confusion. Cerebral inflammation, coma and death could follow within five weeks.

Tripsomotosis is the genus of sleeping sickness reserved for the domestic bovine. So cattle were also absent from the delta. But wild game was immune to the disease, and hence great armies of elephant, buffalo and the large antelope congregated there every year.

Another factor discouraged man, this time a geographical one. The delta is situated many thousands of miles from any settlement of significance, and the areas in between are amongst the most hostile deserts in Africa.

But one group of the earliest black tribesmen who came upon the location were not in awe of this unique natural phenomenon. They had lost their cattle through conquest by another tribe and fled into this strange area. Instead of retracing their steps to join up once more with their tribes-folk, they decided to remain. They learnt to drag thorn bushes through the shallows to catch fish.

They gradually forgot their dependency on cattle. They became immune to tsetse fly and mosquito. They changed their culture to survive and the restless rivers covered their tracks.

"What if that single bloody engine of yours went on the blink?" Montague asked, ignoring the unwritten rule among light plane pilots that such eventualities are never, even frivolously, mentioned.

"No sweat." Weber indicated the radio. "We'd give Smuts our position. At this height, even if the engine cut completely, we'd have 10 minutes of unpowered gliding to find a place to put down. They'd find us before the day was out."

Montague was reassured. Just as long as you didn't hit a tree. But even as he thought thus, he realised Weber would have to search carefully for any vegetation as large as a bush. It had been the last 100 kilometres of the trip that had been the most impressive. Weber had kept his altitude at no more than 3 000 feet, about 1 000 feet above ground level. They saw several herds of elephant browsing in the acacia forests, looking from that height for all the world like a group of fat ticks, the blue kind which dropped off their hosts when they were full of blood, the size of small grapes, and which could probably be voided of their liquid cargo by the equivalent force of a tongue pressed against the palate.

Weber eased the plane downwards. Below, a small airstrip came into view with a tiny windsock flapping idly. The runway ended abruptly in the swamp and Montague was hard put to recognise the fact that the entire countryside was waterlogged apart from the higher ground on which the plane was to land. The sun glinted back in his eyes as the plane banked to come down. What seemed to be grass and solid earth was shown to be weed covered water. Open stretches of lake came into view. A flock of birds whirred off in formation as if their wingtips were threaded together. The strip, hacked out of the bush, was waterlogged after the heavy rain of the previous night. It was not easily apparent from the air that there was a large amount of surface water. Weber was accustomed to this, just one of the several hazards that awaited the inexperienced bush pilot. He watched carefully for indications of rain in the area and he flew low over the strip, carefully searching out the best part. Game on the runway also posed a problem sometime. This was another reason for flying low over the strip, so you could "beat them up" Red lechwe in particular are inclined to stay put unless the aircraft roars a few yards over their heads to announce its intention to land.

Weber had trained himself to make the quick decision go or no go. Almost invariably he decided to go in. The sandy soil was well drained on the whole. Once he committed himself to land, he used the technique of bringing the aircraft in directly and then stopping as quickly as possible. To the unwary passengers, the experience was quite unnerving. The sudden slamming of brakes was like stopping your car against the garage wall. There were puddles on the runway which suddenly appeared in front of them. The whooshing spray of brown water cut visibility to zero, as though the cockpit had been engulfed in a paper bag.

There was an ominous drag to the left and the plane skidded. Weber controlled it with his rudders and brakes. It was as if he were playing tunes on an organ. He concentrated on bringing the craft to a stop quickly, avoiding slipping into a number of holes made by warthog. That could be the worst that could happen breaking the nose wheel. Then the aircraft would flip over.

But as always, he brought them safely to a halt. The only sound that had occurred since he entered into the landing procedure, using full flaps to lose maximum airspeed on the approach, was the strident warning of the stall buzzer as they hit the ground. Weber let the engine run for a few moments before cutting it. Then he opened the door and a draught of hot, moist air engulfed them. The passengers alighted and stretched their legs. Weber handed out the luggage from the hold. Montague moved his jaws to equalise the pressure in his ears.

Weber was flying on to Mongu to fetch Clea and Marshall. He climbed back into the aircraft and the others went to the edge of the airstrip. They watched the plane taxi back to the other end of the cleared runway. It turned and, after a pause, gathered speed and came roaring towards them. Despite the wet conditions, some dust swirled up behind it. Weber waited until the last moment before lifting her off the deck. Then it levelled off once more to gain further power before it finally circled away on its climb to the required altitude.

Several minutes later a Landrover arrived at the airstrip, driven by a young black man in jeans and a tee shirt. He drove them the few hundred yards to the homestead, a distance which they could easily have walked. The air was spiced with the aromatic breath of eucalyptus trees. In one of the garden beds, a voluminous black woman was weeding, a small baby strapped to the broad back. She bent to her task, rocking as she stooped, the child almost upside down but oblivious to the fact that its head was pointing dangerously towards the ground.

The acre sized garden was drenched with shrubs and flowering creepers bougainvillea, Dutchman's Pipe, trumpet vine and potato creeper. Trees shaded the tin roofed building flamboyant, jacaranda, more eucalyptus. What a difference since they were there just a month or two ago, Montague thought. They stood in the shade at the edge of the lawn while the young man went inside to call Itumeleng. The house was surrounded by a wide veranda screened with wire mesh. The sun picked up the dust, insects and decaying flecks of vegetation trapped in the fine mesh.

Tumi came to the door and beckoned them inside. Montague was shocked at her appearance. Her face was not made up, her hair wild and showing more grey than he had remembered. She was wearing a soiled apron.

"You've all come to Ted's funeral. Oh God. Isn't it terrible?" She started sobbing and Darryl went to her to comfort her. He put his arm around her shoulder.

"Where's Clea," she asked between sobs. "I thought you were coming together?"

"She flew up yesterday to Mongu. Weber's gone to fetch her. They'll be back here in half an hour or so," Darryl replied.

"Montague. How good to see you. So they managed to get hold of you in time." She started crying again. "I don't know why I'm like this. It's just seeing you all together. Come in, won't you make some tea. I must get ready. The funeral is in an hour."

They went into the house. Darryl produced a bottle of brandy from the drinks cupboard and placed it on the tea tray. Ted Merryweather's presence still permeated the place. Montague could smell the tobacco he used to smoke and pictured how he used to screw up his eyes against the fumes, those remarkable blue eyes in a face burnt brown by the sun. He picked up an old fob watch that Ted used to carry in a homemade leather pouch on his belt. He wound it up and adjusted the hands to the correct time then replaced it on the sideboard. He opened the window and the breeze fluttered the curtain. The sounds and the smells of the delta floated into the room.

Montague was overwhelmed by a surging grief. His eyes filled with tears. He seemed to watch himself from the outside with half dreaded awareness, grateful in a way because his senses were dulled. It was as though he was under a layer of cotton wool. It insulated him against the pain that was trying to seep up through his bowels. It was a thin but resilient blanket. Perhaps there was a touch of ether in it. He tipped a large portion of brandy into his tea.

They heard the sound of Weber's aircraft returning from Mongu. Montague volunteered to meet the plane at the airstrip, and Tumi indicated the keys of the Landrover hanging from a nail next to the door. He shook his head. "I'll walk down."

"No take it," she insisted. "You'll need it."

He drove to the end of the landing strip and watched as Weber brought the little Cessna in on the strip. Beyond them, the sun glinted off the edge of the lake. The same group of red lechwe were standing knee deep in the water, forming a picturesque tableau. The midday sun reflected off their shiny glossy backs. Suddenly they turned and ran, all together, sending up a rain of water from their hooves. They stopped a little further off and resumed their browsing.

The aircraft landed away from Montague's end of the runway and came to a halt in the distance, then turned slowly, like a miniature, and came creeping back towards him. Montague watched as Weber brought the plane to a halt. He and Marshall alighted. Marshall came towards him. He had a composed look on his face. "Greetings," he said.

Montague watched over the other's shoulder. Weber had taken something out of the hold. It looked like a folding chair. Then he helped Clea out of the small aircraft door. With a tightening of the throat and a wave of dizziness, Montague saw her being placed in what he now recognised as a wheel chair. Weber adjusted a rug on her lap and she approached, propelling the chair herself. Weber stayed behind.

"Watch it," Weber whispered the words so that only Montague could hear him.

Clea smiled and held out her hand. "Hullo, old boy."

"Hullo, Clea. Everything all right?"

"Yes, thank you. All's well. Except Weber thinks there's something wrong with the rudder. Says he'll be along in a jiffy."

"I'll hang on for him," Marshall said. "You two go on ahead. We'll bring the truck."

Montague took the handles of the wheelchair and guided it. He was glad Clea couldn't see that his eyes were filled with tears.

They arrived at the homestead. At the same time Weber and Marshall drove up in the Landrover. Tumi came out the kitchen door. When she saw Clea, she started sobbing again. "He was a good man. Can anyone tell me why he was killed? I found him there, just there. Blood all over his khaki shirt. I couldn't touch him. I wanted to pick him up. But I just couldn't. Someone called up the mission hospital in Mongu and they sent a truck. They just hauled him into the back and drove off." She was getting hysterical. Clea leant forward and took her hand. This comforted her.

"Who would want to kill him?" asked Clea.

Tumi stopped crying. "I don't know what happened," she said. "I was in my bedroom. It was early in the morning. I heard the sound of a truck outside. Then the noise of a door slamming. Then the sound of the engine as it drove off again. I walked slowly to the kitchen. I really didn't think there was anything wrong. I couldn't see Ted. I opened the back door. He was lying on the ground. He had slid down the wall and his head was still upright. But he was dead. I could see that. There was blood everywhere."

Clea persuaded Tumi to lie down for a while. Montague went for a walk by himself. Marshall, Darryl and Weber went for a tour of inspection through the house and outbuildings. Then Denda arrived in a Landrover. Montague came over to greet him.

"Sorry I couldn't be here earlier. Party business."

"Denda, I've been waiting for you," Darryl said. "We still haven't got the whole story."

"Well, the mission doctors could do nothing. He was dead on arrival. They called the police. The death certificate says 'Death by gunshot wound', that's all."

"And the truck that drove up to the house that morning? Has anyone tried to trace that?"

"They've got other priorities," Marshall said.

"Such as?"

"Tracing a whole lot of missing ivory. I was in Mongu this morning. Gordon Mbenya discovered that the bonded store had been burgled. Luckily, he said, only a small quantity had been removed."

"Did Ted know about this?" asked Darryl.

Denda looked at Marshall, then Darryl. "Should he have known anything about it?" he asked.

"No, not necessarily." Marshall was non committal.

"How's Tumi?" Denda asked.

"All right, I think. She's inside with Clea. Why don't you speak to her? I'm sure she'd like to see you. You go and see her too," he said to Montague.

Darryl beckoned Marshall, and they walked over to the outbuildings. "You know what I think? Ted heard that the ivory theft had been discovered."

"You mean someone told him. Could it have been that someone drove down to the homestead that morning to deliver the news and then shot him?"

"I don't think so. My reading is that someone came down in a great hurry to see Ted. Can you remember what Tumi said? She heard the sound of a truck engine. A door slam. And then she heard it drive away again. Does that sound like someone who was planning to kill the old man?"

"He might have planned on getting in and out in the shortest possible time. Hit and run, sort of."

"There's another thing that worries me. Tumi said nothing about the sound of gunshot. That could mean one of two things. Either Ted had been shot earlier on, away from his house and the body was brought back and dumped. That could explain the extreme haste."

"Go on. Or what?"

"Or that Ted had been shot right there, where he was found. But not at that time. Sometime earlier. And the truck driver had come down to tell Ted something, discovered the body, and hightailed if off as fast as he could."

"There's another possibility," said Marshall sombrely. "That is, that Ted took his own life. He realised that the ivory theft could be traced to him, or to his negligence. And he couldn't bear the consequences of his scheme being discovered."

The black priest from the mission conducted the service, alternating between English and Setswana. He had driven down from Mongu with a handful of officials from the Department. Some local villagers and the group of whites clustered round Tumi. Clea held Tumi's hand. Darryl stood on the other side of her.

Montague did not remember any details of the service. They all filed past the grave and dropped handfuls of blossoms on top of the coffin. The wind ruffled the leaves of the blue gum trees and changed the colours of the foliage. Shiny sliver on one side, and flat grey green on the other. It was as though someone drew a wet brush across the tree. It glistened for a moment. Then, just as moisture evaporates when water is flicked onto hot stones, the tree regained its original hue.

He was conscious of the quietness, the peace. The ubiquitous mourning dove, so appropriate, called continuously in the high branches. "Kuk kurrrrru. Kuk kurrrru."

Books by the author:

Footprints in Tzaneen

Footprints in the Lowveld

Footprints in Haenertsburg

Kalahari Dreaming

Matabele Rising

The Baronet and the Savage King

The Infamous Malaboch War and other gripping stories of the old Transvaal

The Saint, the Surgeon and the Unsung Botanist

Books written in collaboration with others:

Bitter Aloes

Hobson's Choice

Judge Pat Tebbutt Remembers

Robert Hart, The first English-speaking settler in South Africa

Salute the Eagle

The Batubatse, their history and tradition

The Diaries of Sapper Robert Poole

The Lucky Bean Tree

The Triumphs, Trials and Tribulations of a Magistrate in the old South Africa

The Wool-classer, the Shearers and the Golden Fleece.